"Katherine . . ." Desire inched aside Aaron's protectiveness as he caught the sultry haze in her eyes. His touch went from comforting to seductive as his fingers tangled in her hair. He wanted to make things right for her. Hell, he wanted her. Period.

One hand fluttered protectively toward her chest, but she didn't push him away. He watched her fingers move in nervous motion against the base of her throat, and ached to press his lips there, see if she tasted as sweet as he imagined.

"Are you an orphan, a murderer, or a magician?" He fingered the lock of hair in order to contain his urge to touch her in places he had no right to touch. "You've certainly cast a spell over me. Who are you, Katherine Jackson?"

"I don't know," she whispered, her eyes shielded by an old pain. She moved his hand away. "I've been looking for the answer to that question all my life."

He glanced at her slender fingers wrapped around his wrist, and cursed himself as his desire for her flared nearly out of control. Damn the consequences. He pressed his body against hers until they were pushed into the soft folds of the red velour. It teased, shimmered behind him as he lowered his mouth to Katherine's ear.

"Then let me help you find out."

WHAT ARE *LOVESWEPT* ROMANCES?

They are stories of true romance and touching emotion. We believe those two very important ingredients are constants in our highly sensual and very believable stories in the LOVESWEPT *line. Our goal is to give you, the reader, stories of consistently high quality that may sometimes make you laugh, sometimes make you cry, but are always fresh and creative and contain many delightful surprises within their pages.*

Most romance fans read an enormous number of books. Those they truly love, they keep. Others may be traded with friends and soon forgotten. We hope that each LOVESWEPT *romance will be a treasure—a "keeper." We will always try to publish*

LOVE STORIES YOU'LL NEVER FORGET
BY AUTHORS YOU'LL ALWAYS REMEMBER

The Editors

BLACK VELVET

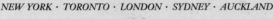

KRISTEN ROBINETTE

BANTAM BOOKS
NEW YORK · TORONTO · LONDON · SYDNEY · AUCKLAND

BLACK VELVET
A Bantam Book / August 1997

ISBN 0-553-44581-2

Published simultaneously in the United States and Canada

Bantam Books are published by Bantam Books, a division of Bantam Doubleday Dell Publishing Group, Inc. Its trademark, consisting of the words "Bantam Books" and the portrayal of a rooster, is Registered in U.S. Patent and Trademark Office and in other countries. Marca Registrada. Bantam Books, 1540 Broadway, New York, New York 10036.

PRINTED IN THE UNITED STATES OF AMERICA

OPM 10 9 8 7 6 5 4 3 2 1

To Mom and Dad,
who gave us wings to fly,
sensible shoes (just in case),
and one another to count on

ONE

Katherine Jackson slipped the receiver back into its cradle with one sticky hand. "Just a wrong number, Roscoe," she said as she licked a blob of chocolate icing from her finger. The fat dachshund at her feet thumped his tail three times in response. One glance at the microwave's clock, which registered 11:58 P.M. in bold red numbers, had told her the call was probably a misdial. No one ever called this late—if anyone called at all.

She pushed a single blue-and-white-striped candle into the brown swirl of icing that now topped a cupcake, struck a match, and touched it to the wick. The acrid smell of sulfur hung in the air as she watched the digital clock. The numbers shifted. Twelve o'clock midnight.

Thirty years old.

"Help me make a wish, Roscoe."

One tan eyebrow arched in the dog's graying black face.

Katherine smiled. "We made that one last year, and look what it got us."

Roscoe lifted his stubby foreleg, resting his callused paw against her bare ankle.

"Okay, but this is the last time." Katherine closed her eyes, made her wish, then blew out the candle.

She recognized him even though she didn't know his name, didn't know who he was. His face was familiar in an odd, welcoming way. In the same way that you recognized your home in the dark of the night, she knew him. Knew she loved him. There was only enough light to define the masculine planes of his face, the slight stubble of dark beard as he leaned closer. She longed to thrust her hands into the thick, wavy hair that fell almost to his shoulders, lose herself in his steady blue gaze. He looked at once young and mature.

Her savior.

Overwhelmed, she tried to look away, but the gentle pressure of his fingers urged her face back toward his. "Stay with me, please."

She had been so frightened before he came, had felt so hopeless. He had changed all that.

He had saved her life.

Emotion threatened to consume her. She loved him with every fiber of her being, yet he was so young. And the pain, the heartache she'd experienced in her life made her old. Too old for him. She tried to remove herself from the fear that threatened to engulf her. She wanted so much to be with him.

"Why won't you stay with me tonight?" His voice was

fading, but he spoke the words with an almost frightening determination.

Katherine struggled to see his face more clearly, understand what was happening. "Wait."

The image of him blurred, and she felt herself being drawn, unwillingly, away. "Wait," she whispered again. "What's your name?"

Through the blurry mist, she saw—or perhaps felt—his hesitation. His brow wrinkled in a look of confusion as he spoke again. "Blake—Owen. Blake."

His image was gone from her then, but a lingering thought echoed in her head. "Scenic View."

Katherine didn't wake quickly. Instead she lay very still, willing the image to return. The emotions that had left her body trembling were bittersweet. A love as she'd never experienced had penetrated her to the bone. And grief at their parting had exhausted her, leaving her devoid of any emotion other than the turmoil that still swirled about her.

Finally she swung her feet over the edge of the bed, then stopped to massage her temples. Unshed tears filled her eyes, and she couldn't resist pulling her pillow into her lap for a reassuring hug. Slowly the familiar surroundings of her bedroom gave her a welcome sense of reality.

Sunlight streamed through the wooden blinds and fell in patches against the old quilt that lay at the foot of her bed. Houseplants adorned every flat surface, including her antique bureau. One wayward vine had begun to climb from its terra-cotta pot on the floor and up the iron bed frame.

She swallowed hard, allowing the comfort of the rambling old apartment to work its magic. Still, the dream images wouldn't fade. "Wow," she whispered into the early-morning quiet of the room.

Katherine couldn't honestly say she'd looked forward to her thirtieth birthday, but the dream had been some weird reaction, all right. She pulled her robe across her shoulders and shrugged into the thin silk. Funny, she didn't feel any older. What she did feel, though, was lonely. An emotion she should have been used to, but wasn't.

Odd, she mused, how you formed ideas of what life was supposed to be like at a certain age. In her visions of her thirtieth birthday, there had been a toddler sitting in her lap, helping her blow out the candles.

She shook her head to clear the thought. *You've got to play the hand you're dealt.* That's what Grams always said.

But the dream had been so real, and so exhausting, the pain of separation almost unbearable. And to top it off, she'd cast herself as the older woman in the dream. She wrinkled her nose. How Freudian. Birthday anxiety. It might as well be written in blinking neon above her head.

Katherine cast the pillow aside with an irritated shove and turned to stare at her disheveled image in the bureau mirror. Sleepy green eyes looked back at her from a too-pale face, while a lopsided ponytail sprayed a mass of dark brown hair from atop her head.

She flicked the cascade of hair over her shoulder. Still herself. But in the surreal way of dreams, she *had* been herself, yet also someone else. Someone older, she thought. And much sadder.

Roscoe interrupted her thoughts as he waddled out from under the bed, his back barely skimming the iron frame. He absently licked her bare toes before heading down the hall toward the kitchen.

"Hey, you," she called after him. "You ate all the plain cupcakes, and you know what happened last time you ate a chocolate one."

Roscoe stopped and looked back at her, his thick tail beating a hollow cadence against the old plaster of the apartment's hallway. He had a thing for chocolate. But chocolate, she'd learned the hard way, had it in for dogs.

"Kibbles for you, coffee for me," she promised. "Just give me a minute."

After a quick shower and a trip outside with Roscoe, Katherine found herself sipping an indulgent third cup of coffee and staring at the phone book. The advertisement for the Scenic View Inn was small. She ran her finger over the words "Tennessee's best-kept secret." She had been relatively certain that there was actually an inn by that name, but recent growth had inched out some of the older places.

Muted voices penetrated the silence of the kitchen, and below her second-floor apartment, a car's trunk closed with a thud.

Katherine stuck a pen in the crease of the phone book and slammed it shut. Grams and Walt were headed to Virginia to visit their son and new grandson. She hopped up and crossed to the window that overlooked the street. Walt, typically dressed in a Hawaiian shirt and dress slacks, was stuffing an ice chest into the back of Grams's old kelly-green Buick. Walt wasn't one to get too far away from the fridge, even if it meant he had to take it with him.

Grams, on the other hand, was standing statue-still, staring up at Katherine's window.

Katherine waved, then opened the heavy window and stuck her upper body out into the warm summer air.

"You knew I wanted to say good-bye, didn't you?" Grams called from below.

Katherine couldn't help but smile. Grams was forever trying to convince her she was psychic. She had to admit that she had a sometimes uncanny and always annoying habit of knowing more than she was supposed to. But psychic? No. Maybe it would be good for Grams's health food store, though, if she were. *Come visit our psychic store clerk.* It had a nice ring to it.

"Yes," she answered. "But I knew the old-fashioned way. I heard Walt slam the trunk."

Grams cast an adoring look at her husband before remembering to scowl. "We should have been gone over an hour ago." She waved her hand in Walt's direction, then stopped to sniff the air. "I smell coffee." She turned and sniffed in earnest, as if searching for the source of the offending aroma. "Katherine, do you smell coffee?"

Katherine stole a guilty glance toward her coffee

cup. "Yes, I believe I do." She pretended to adjust her heavy ponytail while she thought. Finally she gestured toward the old two-story frame house that mirrored the house she shared with Grams and Walt. "Maybe Mrs. Panopoulos is brewing some." She wrinkled her nose for effect.

Below her, Grams shook her head. "Maybe so. Why anyone would drink that horrible stuff when they could have a nice cup of chamomile tea, is beyond me."

Katherine gave a noncommittal nod and pretended to swat a fly.

"Honey, I'm sorry we're leaving on your birthday of all days, but—"

"Hey, don't worry about it. I'd say it's perfect timing no matter when a baby arrives."

Grams smiled up at her. "I guess you're right about that. Well, we'd best be off. I'll call and check on you when we get there."

"Okay, and Walt—" The older man looked up suddenly, probably unaware that she'd been talking with Grams. Katherine shook her head. At least maybe he'd packed his hearing aid, since he refused to wear it. "Kiss that new grandson for me." The words squeaked out around the lump in her throat, as she found herself fighting a fear that was almost as old as she was.

Walt blew her a dramatic kiss, no doubt pretending he'd actually heard what she'd said. "Happy birthday, sweetheart. See you soon."

The lump in her throat doubled, and all she could manage was a wave before she closed the window. It wasn't logical, the fear she felt at the sight of Walt and Grams leaving.

Katherine closed her eyes, but all she could see was the cloud of dust streaming out from behind her daddy's pickup truck. It was the last time she'd seen him. She had been eight years old at the time. The following month she'd turned nine.

No, she'd turned bitter.

Grams, despite the nickname, wasn't her grandmother at all. She and Walt were her foster parents. Her third set, in fact. Things had been different—she had been different—when she'd first come to them. Katherine recalled the weary, defeated child she'd been at fourteen, and shivered despite the sunlight that bathed her arms through the window. She couldn't imagine what her life would have turned out like if Grams and Walt hadn't opened their home and their hearts. . . .

She unclenched her fists and opened her eyes. Vacation. That was her problem. She hated vacation. Too much time on her hands. But Grams always insisted she take vacation whenever Grams and Walt did, leaving her with nothing to do. She turned back to the table and opened the phone book, absently circling the advertisement for the Scenic View Inn.

The sudden awareness of him—of the man in her dreams—was at once sweet and painful. Familiar and confusing. The feelings were so real, so tangible, she could reach out and touch them, touch him. . . .

She threw her hands into the air. It had been a dream, for heaven's sake. She was bored already, that's all there was to it. Go check the ginseng plants—that's what she should do. Grams had made it her personal mission to see the American version of the rare wild plant cultivated and preserved. Katherine sighed. That would only take an hour or two, but at least it was something productive to do.

The prospect of the next week loomed before her like a lonely stretch of road. She stretched her long legs beneath the kitchen table and wiggled her bare toes. She took another sip of coffee, and a wicked smile spread across her face. What could it hurt? Vacation was supposed to be fun, right?

She'd check the plants. Right after she called the Scenic View Inn.

Katherine checked the phone book and dialed the inn's number before she could change her mind. Just something fun to do, just something to kill a little—

"Good morning. Scenic View Inn. May I assist you?"

Her coffee mug hit the table with a thud. What was she thinking, playing on the phone like a mischievous child? But now that she'd actually dialed the number, she couldn't hang up in the woman's face. Okay—she'd just ask for him, then the switchboard operator would tell her that no such person was registered, and she would politely thank her and hang up. That's what she'd do.

Katherine cleared her throat. "Uh . . . yes. I was wondering if you had a guest by the name of Blake Owen registered?"

"One moment and I'll check."

She ran the tips of her fingers against the ancient wood of her kitchen table, absently wondering who had made the scars that were now part of the surface.

"Ma'am?"

Katherine jumped as if she'd been shot. How long had she been sitting there? "Yes. I'm still here."

"I'm sorry, we don't have a Blake Owen registered with us."

Of course they didn't. He was a figment of her imagination. Her dream man. Katherine almost laughed out loud, more than a little relieved to end the conversation. "Thank you anyway—"

"But we do have an Owen Blake."

Blake—Owen. Blake. The words swirled around in her head.

The woman's businesslike voice interrupted, bringing her back to the present. "He's in room 315. Shall I connect you?"

"No!" The word left her mouth too fast, too harshly. "No, thank you," she amended. "He's . . . He's not expecting my call."

"Got it!" Detective Aaron Stone clasped the startled switchboard operator on the shoulder. "555-5309," he said aloud as he wrote the numbers down in his left-handed scrawl. Setting up the tracing equipment had been a hunch, one Lieutenant Dawson hadn't wanted to authorize. Aaron stared at the number in his hand. Score one for harassing the lieutenant.

He handed the scrap of paper to Johnny Jacobs, a rookie whose wide-eyed enthusiasm reminded him of his own when he'd joined the force. "Get me a name and address to go with this."

"Right away, Detective." Johnny trotted off toward the pay phone in the hotel's lobby.

Aaron ran his hand over his chin—over two days' worth of stubble there—as he watched the rookie officer. "Off to save the world, aren't you?" he mumbled.

The switchboard operator looked up at him. "Did you say something?"

"No, nothing important. Thank you for your help this morning." She'd handled the call like a pro. "Will you be available if I need you again?"

"Yes, of course." Aaron thought he detected a slight blush beneath the middle-aged woman's thick makeup.

Her willingness to help made him slightly ashamed of his bad attitude. He had to admit that his cynicism was at a high peak that morning. He popped a stick of cinnamon chewing gum in his mouth and rubbed his burning eyes.

Sleeping in a dead man's hotel room was enough to give anybody nightmares, but that damned dream he'd had the night before beat all. Stakeouts weren't his thing, but dredging up the past was even lower on the list. It had been several years since she'd haunted his dreams, and even longer since he'd been able to envision her with such clarity. But last night he could have reached out and touched her. Last night he—

"Detective?"

Aaron turned to face an eager Johnny Jacobs, and almost laughed at the triumphant look on the kid's face. "So tell me the name of our prime suspect, Johnny. Or at least who can tell us why Owen Blake left here yesterday in a body bag." He tossed the gum wrapper in the rookie's direction.

To his surprise the kid caught it like a seasoned shortstop, then tossed it into the switchboard operator's trash can before he answered.

"Katherine Jackson. 1121 Mockingbird Lane."

TWO

The wind curled over the edge of the convertible, standing Roscoe's long ears on end. Katherine stole a glance in his direction as she accelerated. Every time she allowed her plump little roommate to ride with her, she knew why she had chosen to restore the car. Despite his age, Roscoe stuck his sharp muzzle into the wind and took a bite out of his invisible opponent.

"What on God's green earth am I doing?" she whispered as she pulled the Cutlass into the parking lot of the Scenic View Inn.

She found a parking space that was shaded by an oak tree and backed in. Suddenly nervous, she readjusted her sunglasses on her nose. She should be cleaning her apartment. She should be checking the ginseng plants. Heck, she should be doing anything except chasing ghosts. The image of steel-blue eyes and thick, dark hair flashed in her head. If this Owen Blake character wanted to haunt her dreams, that was fine with her. What woman in her right mind would complain?

The real question was: What woman in her right mind would think, even for a moment, that he actually existed?

Well, what harm would it do? She and Roscoe were just out for a midday drive, after all. If she happened to see the man of her dreams going in or out of the inn, that would be great.

Yeah, right. She stifled a laugh. That would mean something else entirely. It would mean she was a nut, or worse, a nut who was so bored, she was hallucinating. Darker memories threatened to surface at that thought, but Katherine firmly pushed them aside.

She pulled a fast-food sack from the backseat and removed two hamburgers. A quick check told her which was Roscoe's—a bun, hamburger patty, and cheese. Hers, on the other hand, was loaded. She pulled back the wrapping. Grams would have a fit. Double cheese, pickles, special sauce—

"Katherine Jackson?" The voice, deep and slightly gruff, came from beside her.

Startled, she hastily rewrapped her hamburger as her gaze traced one of the most heart-stopping male bodies she'd ever seen. Khaki chinos hugged athletic hips, and a rumpled white button-down shirt was opened at the collar, revealing a wide *V* of tanned chest that was swirled with dark hair. She stopped at his face, and her heart began to dance so erratically, she felt faint. Sunglasses hid his eyes, but she recognized the dark stubble that covered his square chin, the thick black hair that fell to his collar in wavy disarray. . . .

Owen Blake was standing next to her car.

"Are you Katherine Jackson?" The voice repeated

the question, but another question whispered to her. *"Why won't you stay with me tonight?"*

No doubt about it, it was the same voice. The same man. No doubt about it, she was going crazy.

He removed his sunglasses. "Ma'am?"

The same steady blue eyes from her dream were looking down at her, except this time . . . this time they weren't kind. She removed her own sunglasses and placed a comforting hand on Roscoe, who was more interested in eating his hamburger than noticing that a figment of her imagination had just sprung to life.

"Yes, I'm Katherine Jackson."

"I'm Detective Aaron Stone with the Chattanooga Police."

No, you're not, she wanted to say. *You're Owen Blake.*

"Would you mind stepping out of the car?" He motioned to someone over his shoulder. "I'd like to ask you some questions."

Her head was spinning. What was going on? What could she have possibly done that the police wanted to question her about? None of this was even possible.

Finally, she found her voice. "No. I mean— No, I don't mind, but I don't understand. What do you want to question me about?"

She opened the door and stood. Katherine was tall, but he—Detective, he'd said? Detective Stone. He was at least three inches taller. She felt trapped between his body and the car, and for a moment all she could think about was his nearness—this man, the man from her dream.

He replaced his sunglasses, extinguishing the

warmth she'd found in his eyes—or at least the warmth she remembered from last night. He cleared his throat, and she noticed a muscle in his jaw jumped before he spoke.

"I want to question you regarding the death of Owen Blake."

Aaron watched her face, or more specifically, watched the blood drain from it. He'd blurted out the words to gauge her reaction, and he'd gotten what he wanted. In fact, he thought she was going to faint. But she didn't. Instead she just stood there, her wide green eyes staring a hole through him, not moving an inch.

She may not have killed him herself, but judging from the look on her face, Aaron didn't doubt for a minute that she knew what had happened to Owen Blake.

"Were you acquainted with the deceased?"

Her hand went to her throat, but she didn't make a sound.

Johnny Jacobs joined them, standing next to Aaron. Aaron turned to him. "Miss Jackson has agreed to answer some questions. Would you mind taking notes?"

He looked back at Katherine. "Let me ask you again, Miss Jackson. Did you know Owen Blake?"

She shook her head as if denying something, more to herself than to him. "No, I didn't." She reached for the car's door handle.

Her hair was pulled up, fastened with some type of clasp at the crown, and a few loose strands played about her face as she shook her head. Aaron felt a surge of disappointment. Someone with the face of an angel had no business being involved with drug-dealing scum like

Owen Blake. He ground the heel of his boot against the concrete, a habit carried over from his smoking days.

He met her eyes again, knowing his own were shielded by the tint of his sunglasses, preferring it that way. She wore no makeup. His eyes quickly scanned the interior of her car before returning to her body. She wore no bra beneath her gray T-shirt either. That was a fact he'd made quick note of before the professional in him had gone to work, had asked the question he knew would damn her.

He'd wanted her to say yes, that she knew Owen Blake. He could have been her brother, a friend. She could have not known that he was dead. But she did. There was no other explanation for the guilty, confused expression on her perfect alabaster face.

But why was she sitting, exposed, in a convertible at the scene of the crime? No, even better, in a convertible, feeding a hamburger to a dog. What in the hell were those dogs called, anyway? His mind was blank. Still, he refused to write "wiener dog" on the report.

But at the moment he was faced with another problem. Miss Katherine Jackson thought she was about to drive away. He caught her wrist just as she opened the car door, and his arm brushed against the side of her breast. He lost himself for a moment, felt the undeniable tightening of his upper thighs that preceded arousal.

Women weren't women in situations like this, he reminded himself. They were criminals. Even this one.

"I'm afraid we have evidence to the contrary, Miss Jackson." He tightened his grip on her wrist. "I need for you to come down to the station and answer a few more questions."

To his surprise, the expression on her face went from guilty to angry. She jerked her arm away, her green eyes suddenly infused with light. "Am I under arrest?"

Damn. She either knew he couldn't hold her without a warrant, or was playing a hunch of her own. He was itching to question her right away, to see how easily she'd give up what she knew. He allowed the silence to stretch between them, a little theatrical tactic he used occasionally to measure reaction. This time, though, he found his own mind drifting, wondering if she knew the shape of her nipples was outlined beneath the thin fabric of her T-shirt, if she was aware of her striking looks at all. Something told him she wasn't.

He ground another invisible cigarette beneath his foot and forced himself to focus on the situation. There were less obvious ways of finding out what she was up to, and they might prove to be more revealing.

"No. You're free to go."

Aaron sensed Johnny's surprise. He met the rookie's eyes and shook his head in silent signal. Johnny would get his chance to pursue this case, probably sooner than he wanted. And probably for longer than he wanted, Aaron thought. The corners of his mouth twitched with a suppressed smile. An all-night surveillance assignment ought to take some of the perk out of his perky little butt.

The dog—dachshund, that was it—seemed oblivious to the tension as Katherine got back into the car. She scooted him over patiently, but Aaron noticed her fingers were trembling as she started to turn the key in the ignition. She looked up at him with what was the most sincere expression he'd ever seen on a suspect's face, or at least the best acting job he'd seen in ages.

"I don't know anything about this man's death." She spread her fingers against the steering wheel and closed her eyes briefly. When she opened them again, Aaron thought he glimpsed a glimmer of tears. "And I don't know how to make you believe me."

Aaron saw the golden opportunity he'd been looking for and decided to use it, to cut straight to the chase. He leaned against the convertible's door and spoke slowly. "Why did you call the Scenic View Inn this morning?"

He heard the sharp intake of her breath as her lips parted. The indecision on her face was obvious. Finally she spoke. No, whispered.

"I had a dream last night." She stifled a nervous laugh and ran her hand across her face. "Never mind."

She cranked the old Cutlass then, and Aaron straightened. He couldn't help but appreciate her taste in cars. The engine purred, smooth but powerful. A classic, just like the woman driving it.

A classic liar.

"Wait," he called as she started to pull forward. She stopped the car, looking expectantly at his face. "What do you mean, you had a dream? What does that have to do with anything?"

She put her sunglasses on and shook her head. "Nothing. You wouldn't believe me, anyway. It's just that I couldn't shake this dream. . . ." She faced forward again. "Like I said, you wouldn't understand."

He watched the black Cutlass move slowly through the hotel parking lot and disappear onto the parkway. With last night as a cruel reminder, he knew about strange dreams. Dreams about people, things, better off forgotten.

He turned to Johnny. "What are you doing tonight?"

Johnny straightened his holster. "Pulling a double. Sergeant has me assigned to Roadie's."

Aaron mentally cursed his decision to allow Katherine Jackson to go. Roadie's Bar had been nothing but trouble for the last three weeks. There was no way in hell he could convince the sergeant to pull Jacobs off it.

"Why are you pulling a double? Is the precinct shorthanded?"

Johnny looked at him like he'd just landed in a spaceship. "It's the Fourth of July holiday this week. Vacation's at a premium, and a summer bug's going around to boot."

"Ah, hell!"

Johnny smirked. "You have heard of it, haven't you? Independence Day?"

"Yes, I've heard of it." Aaron ignored Johnny's attempt to goad him. He'd forgotten all about the holiday. His parents, not to mention all five of his siblings and their assorted offspring, would be expecting him at his brother David's house. Well, this year they might have to celebrate without him.

It looked like he was going to have something else to do. And that something else involved keeping a close eye on one beautiful, guilty-as-hell brunette.

21

Katherine turned the key, and the dead bolt snapped with a loud crack. Her hands trembling, she pushed open the heavy glass door to the Herb Shop. Grams wouldn't approve, of course, but working was the only way to save her sanity. She switched on the lights, and the fluorescent fixtures illuminated row after row of carefully stocked herbs and vitamins, natural medicines and toiletries.

Walking through the door to the shop was as close to getting a hug from Grams as possible. The store was a reflection of Grams, of the gentle, nurturing soul and astute businesswoman that made her who she was.

Not much needed to be done, but darn it, she'd find something. Katherine pulled out an inventory list she'd been working on, and turned on the computer. She'd get him out of her mind if it was the last thing she did. The inventory list hit the countertop with a thud.

The police wanted to question her regarding a man's death, and all she could think about was the man from her dream. A man was dead, for heaven's sake, and logical or not, she was involved.

The entrance bell jangled, and Katherine looked up to see several boxes enter the door. She smiled. Beneath them, she was certain, was Cheryl Simpson. Cheryl ran the diner next door to the Herb Shop, and often signed for deliveries if Katherine and Grams were not available.

"Hey," a squeaky voice called out. Cheryl had the most exaggerated Southern accent Katherine had ever heard, and that was saying something, considering she'd never been north of Tennessee.

Katherine hopped down from the counter stool, crossed to the door, and looked down on Cheryl's head. "May I help you?" she asked, unable to resist teasing her friend. Cheryl was as feisty as they came, and Katherine wouldn't put a shin-kick past her.

"Yes, you may." Cheryl shifted the packages. "And in the next ten seconds, unless you want these all over the floor."

Katherine easily lifted the top box from Cheryl's load. "What happened, did you scare the parcel delivery guy again?"

Cheryl stacked the second box in Katherine's arms. "If I wasn't married to the best cook in Tennessee, I'd do more than scare him."

Katherine laughed for the first time in what felt like forever. She'd been desperate to shake the scene that had been running through her head all day, the image of Owen Blake—Detective Stone—leaning over the door of her car. She barely suppressed a shiver. The accusation in his eyes still made her blood run cold. She set the boxes down and rubbed her arms, hoping Cheryl wouldn't recognize the myriad of emotions behind the sudden gesture.

She looked up to find Cheryl eyeing her, curiosity written all over her face. And Cheryl's curiosity was relentless. Katherine needed an out, something to deflect the question that she knew was on the tip of her friend's tongue.

She pasted on a quick smile and pointed to a round colorful button pinned to Cheryl's blouse. "What does that say?" She leaned forward and read, "Ask me about my new basil biscuits."

Cheryl frowned with distrust. "Yeah, one of James's new creations. Say, is anything—?"

Katherine laughed. "For a minute I thought it said, 'Ask me about my new baby.' "

Cheryl's brown eyes went round as saucers, and every freckle stood out against her fair skin like a neon sign. Katherine knew right away that she'd done it again.

"Who told you—?" Cheryl cupped her cheeks as her eyes moistened. "Oh, I swear Mother can't keep a secret to save her life."

A shriek of delight escaped Katherine before she drew Cheryl into a hug. "You're going to have a baby?"

Cheryl nodded, a grin spreading across her face.

"I'm so happy for you and James," Katherine said as her mind raced ahead. How was she going to explain this one?

"You're not mad at me for not telling you? I would have, but . . . Well, the truth is I'm not a spring chicken anymore, and I wanted to make sure everything went well." She placed a protective hand over her stomach. "You know, let a little time pass before I told anyone."

"Of course I'm not angry." Though she was tempted, it wasn't fair to let Cheryl believe that her mother had spilled the beans. "But don't be mad at your mom. I didn't know about the baby."

She met Cheryl's suspicious look with an even gaze. "I didn't—honestly. It was just a coincidence."

One of many, Katherine thought. It seemed she was

constantly explaining herself—choosing the right words to explain why it appeared she was privy to other people's secrets, feeling guilty for somehow knowing the details of their lives that she logically shouldn't know.

Frankly, she was tired of walking around with her foot in her mouth. Though she'd tried to convince herself otherwise over the years, the truth was becoming painfully obvious. She knew things, things she shouldn't know. What she didn't know, was how to keep her mouth shut about it.

The thoughts seemed to pop out at the worst possible times. Usually when her guard was down, she realized. The image of Owen Blake—Aaron Stone—invaded her mind. His breath warm against her cheek as he begged her to stay, his voice deep and filled with love for her. Or at least for the woman she'd been last night.

Yes, her guard had been down in that case, all right. She'd been asleep.

Her gaze was suddenly drawn over Cheryl's shoulder, toward the section of street visible through the glass door. A murky tan sedan was parked across the street from the shop. She would have known it was Detective Stone even if he'd bothered to be less obvious.

". . . you know James and I thought we'd never be able to have kids."

Cheryl's voice penetrated her thoughts, and Katherine forced herself to look away from the car. Away from Aaron Stone.

"Are you okay?" Cheryl glanced over her shoulder toward the street. "You look like you've seen a ghost."

Katherine thought back on the patient blue eyes of the man in her dream. Aaron Stone's eyes, she corrected herself. She felt as if someone were twisting her heart. God, how he'd loved her, needed her. Her face flushed hot. How he'd begged her to stay with him.

Aaron Stone was the man from her dream. There was no more denying it—not unless she was willing to believe that she was losing her mind. And she wasn't willing to go down that road again. Once, with her mother, had been enough.

She snapped her gaze back to Cheryl. "I'm fine." She straightened her shoulders and smiled. "And you and the baby are going to be fine too. James must be ecstatic."

Cheryl checked her watch and groaned. "More like furious right now." She wrinkled her nose. "I left him with a restaurant full of hungry folks."

Katherine stole a quick glance out the door. Detective Stone was still out there, one arm slung outside the open car window, his gaze fixed undeniably on her.

She walked with Cheryl to the door. "Well, I'll just bet you're easily forgiven these days."

Cheryl patted Katherine on the arm and winked. "Being forgiven is how I got in this condition in the first place."

The entrance bell rang as Cheryl scooted out the door. With a quick wave she was gone, leaving Katherine staring through the glass—returning the unflinching stare of Aaron Stone.

The way she saw it, she had two options. She could

either believe in herself, in whatever bizarre ability she possessed, or she could believe she was crazy. A hazy, time-altered image of her mother flashed before her eyes.

No. She wasn't crazy. That possibility was too horrible to even consider. Some people had abilities, didn't they? Whatever weird, psychic connection she'd made with Aaron Stone the night before was real. As real as the man who watched her from across the street.

Katherine straightened the summer sweater she wore. Gone were the T-shirt and shorts from that morning. She'd taken Roscoe home and changed into a sleeveless sweater and colorful broomstick skirt and sandals before coming to the shop. She took a deep breath and reminded herself that she'd done nothing wrong.

"I haven't done anything wrong, and I'm not crazy," she whispered. If it came down to it, she'd find a way to convince Aaron Stone of those facts.

And she had a feeling it was about to come down to it.

She pushed open the door and headed across the street. She was midway there when he stepped out of his car. The plain, official-looking sedan was such a drab backdrop to the man who emerged that it was almost comical. He was anything but drab. The five-o'clock shadow had been shaved clean, the wrinkled chinos and shirt replaced by snug black denims and an olive-green crew-necked shirt.

She shouldn't have been surprised that he got out of the car. He struck her as the type who had to be in charge of every situation. Katherine shook her head. If he thought his size would intimidate her, he was mistaken.

The closer she got, though, the less certain she was of that. His hair was damp, and the soft, spicy aroma of soap told her he had just showered. Dark strands of hair clung to one another and fell to his shoulders with just the right amount of curl. A woman would kill for that hair, she thought absently, not to mention the long black lashes that framed his light blue eyes.

Those eyes, along with a cocky, amused grin, spoke volumes about his opinion of her. She placed her hands on her hips in an effort to maintain her confidence. She had nothing to feel guilty about. Absolutely nothing.

"Detective Stone," she said as she stopped in front of him.

"Miss Jackson," he drawled with maddening sarcasm.

"Is there something I can do for you?" As soon as the words were out, she knew she had set herself up for an answer she wasn't going to like.

He folded his arms across his chest, and a distracting play of muscle moved beneath his tanned skin. "Well, let's see now . . . For starters, you can tell me how you knew Owen Blake."

"I didn't know Owen Blake," she fired back.

He leaned toward her, his eyes boring into hers, his face just inches from her own. She was assaulted by his nearness, by the familiar sight of his face so close to hers. *Why won't you stay with me tonight?* The words were like a drug, like some crazy déjà vu that made her head swim. Her lips were dry, her mind blank.

"You called the Scenic View Inn and asked for Owen Blake. We traced your number, Miss Jackson."

Her head was swimming, and she struggled to remember why she'd felt it necessary to confront him in the first place.

"Look, I had a dream. Okay? Simple as that. A weird dream about a man named Owen Blake. I remembered the name of the hotel from my dream this morning, so I called. It was just a lark—something to do."

Aaron hesitated, then looked pointedly at the Herb Shop. "And now I'm supposed to believe you're some kind of psychic?"

"No, you're not supposed to believe anything. I never expected you to. It's just a strange coincidence."

He tucked the tips of his fingers into his jeans pockets and rocked back on his heels. "Good, because I sleep better at night when I operate on the facts."

Katherine sent up a quick prayer for patience. Holding her temper in check had never been her strong suit. "Good. Then prove I had something to do with Owen Blake's death."

He looked her up and down, paused, then took a second look. A smile played slowly across his face. "I intend to."

She folded her arms across her breasts. "And how do you intend to do that?"

"Oh, the truth has a way of coming out. All I have to do is be around when it does."

"Considering I'm innocent, you may be hanging around for a while."

"Okay by me." He gestured toward the cloudless

sky. "It's a nice day"—he looked directly back at her—"and the scenery is great."

"We can both do without your sarcasm."

There wasn't any humor in his eyes. "Then tell me what you know."

Katherine was weary. The heat rising from the asphalt was making her light sweater feel like a wool blanket, and her panties and bra were sticking to her like a damp second skin. She shook her head, the seed of a headache sprouting behind her eyes. "I have work to do." She turned and crossed to the other side of the street.

"Katherine?"

She shouldn't have stopped. She knew it as soon as her feet faltered on the pavement, but the sound of his voice calling her name blasted through her determination to leave. She turned to face him, feeling defeated already.

"What was the dream about?"

The road was between them, and a car passed by at breakneck speed, its wind lifting the long hem of her skirt. She cupped her hand over her eyes to shield them from the sun's glare. "What? What possible difference could it make—?"

"I want to know."

"He was just a man I knew." She shook her head, then raised her voice to be heard across the street. "Actually I didn't know who he was, but in the dream I . . ."

"Go on." The two simple words made her jump.

"I loved him." A couple stared in her direction as they walked by. "This is ridiculous."

A second car whizzed by. After it passed, Aaron crossed the road at a jog.

He stopped before her and placed his hands on his hips. The material of his shirt pulled across his chest, and Katherine noticed he was breathing hard.

"And?"

"He wanted me to stay, and I couldn't—"

"Why?" He almost barked the word.

She planted her hands on her hips as well, raising her chin to look into his eyes. "What difference does it make?"

"What else, dammit? Why couldn't you stay?"

He ought to find this part amusing, Katherine thought. She raised her eyebrows and her voice. "He was too young for me."

Detective Stone's eyes narrowed, and his face hardened into a mask of barely checked anger. He muttered something under his breath and turned away. She wasn't sure what emotions were responsible for the expression on his face, but amusement wasn't one of them.

"What is it?" she asked.

When he turned toward her again, her breath caught in her throat. The suspicious look on his face was the same, but something had changed. Drastically.

"Go on," he said slowly.

She wasn't sure if she was more frightened of continuing or of disregarding the command. In the end, she decided to seize the opportunity to tell the truth, to tell her side of the story no matter how bizarre it might seem. At least she had his attention.

"The man in my dream saved my life—I'm not sure

how. He wanted me to be with him, but I couldn't go. He was younger than me, and—"

Detective Stone jerked her arm against his chest faster than Katherine could react. "Is that supposed to unnerve me?" His breath was hot and rapid against her ear as he growled out the words. "So you have contacts in the department. That doesn't change a damn thing as far as I'm concerned."

He pulled back to stare into her face. His eyes were dark, the only light left in them dimmed to an angry glow. He lowered his mouth near hers, and for a crazy moment she thought he was going to kiss her. Instead he broke his gaze from hers and looked over her shoulder.

He loosened his grip, and Katherine heard the unmistakable sound of footsteps passing behind them. Slowly, with excruciating tenderness, he caressed the side of her face. "If I find you snooping around in my past again, I'll do more than just keep an eye on you."

He dropped his hand and stepped back.

"That, Katherine Jackson, is a promise."

THREE

Katherine switched on the bedside lamp and sat up. As much as she wanted it, sleep wasn't going to arrive anytime soon. She rubbed her wrist, eyeing the pale blue mark that encircled it. Anger coiled inside her, anger with Aaron Stone and with herself.

He'd just turned and walked away after manhandling her. But she was the one who'd let him.

Now here she sat with a million words of rebuttal, a thousand ways she wished she'd reacted churning in her mind. He'd been furious with her. Furious that she'd meddled in his past. She shook her head and grabbed a book from her nightstand. She didn't have a clue as to what he'd been talking about, but she didn't doubt for a minute that he was convinced she did.

Since there was nothing between them but the investigation—and the dream, she reminded herself—his suspicions had to be tied to one or the other. Her gut told her that it was the dream.

She opened the romance novel, but closed her eyes

instead of reading, allowing her head to sink back into the soft down of her pillow.

Stay with me, please. The words echoed in her head, sweet and tempting.

She almost dreaded the possibility of the dream returning. Almost. She took a deep breath and forced herself to relax for the first time all day.

A sharp scraping sound echoed against the hardwood floor of her apartment. She jerked upright, her fingers pressing against the unread pages of her novel, her heart pounding against her chest. Had she been asleep? A nervous glance at her bedside clock told her she had been asleep for nearly an hour. So much for her insomnia.

She slid out of her bed and looked beneath its iron frame. Nothing but empty space stared back at her. Where was Roscoe? She started to call out for him, but intuition told her to wait. A second sound, this time a dull thud, came from the interior of the apartment.

She froze, listening. The kitchen. Katherine instantly recognized the way the sound echoed down the long hall that joined the apartment's two bedrooms to the kitchen. Her heart leaped in her chest as a second scraping noise was followed by what could have been a whispered curse.

Instinct took over. She sent up a quick prayer of thanks for the dimmer switch on the lamp that silently faded the bedside light to pitch blackness. She lifted the cordless phone from its cradle and slipped beneath the bed. The eerie green glow from the phone's dial face illuminated her shaking fingers as she pressed the emergency button.

"Nine-one-one," an official voice responded immediately. "May I assist you?"

Katherine hesitated. What if she was wrong? What if it was only Roscoe banging around in the kitchen? She hesitated for only a moment, though. Her instincts had never let her down. In fact, it was probably the only thing she'd been able to count on over the years.

"I think there's someone in my apartment." She measured the whispered volume of her words with sheer terror. She might have only seconds. She had to make sure the operator heard her, but if the intruder heard her . . . "I'm at 1121—"

"I have your address on my screen, but let me confirm. Are you at 1121 Mockingbird Lane?"

"Yes," she whispered, thankful for the operator's quick assessment of her need to be silent, and for every square inch of space that separated her bedroom from the kitchen. She would never complain about vacuuming the big old apartment again.

"Hang on. I'm dispatching someone right now." There was a clamor of background noise, muted voices and the anxious sound of static, before the woman's reassuring voice returned. "Can you tell me what room of your house you're in?"

"Upstairs." Katherine stopped short as she heard the unmistakable sound of footsteps in the hall. She took a chance and whispered one last word, knowing—praying—it might make the difference. "Bedroom."

Aaron readjusted his back against the curve of the car's interior. Economical was one thing, torture was another. The Naugahyde squeaked in protest at the motion. Sitting in the department-issued car was about as much fun as being buried in a pine box. He pulled a thermos of coffee from underneath the seat and unscrewed the lid.

It had been a couple of years since he'd had to pull routine surveillance. He'd not only been younger then, he'd been willing. Now his eyes burned with the struggle to stay awake, and his shoulders were in dire need of a rubdown. Or at least, in his case, a hot, soothing shower.

He stifled a tired laugh. Maybe the fact that the car's interior was so uncomfortable was more than a coincidence. He sloshed black coffee into the thermos's plastic lid. He would have nodded off hours ago otherwise.

The car's radio interrupted his brooding. "Car fifty-four. We have a burglary in progress. 1121 Mockingbird Lane. Can you respond?"

"Damn." Aaron's curse was punctuated by a hot splash of coffee against his denim-covered leg. He shoved the cup onto the car's dashboard and barely remembered to snatch up the radio receiver.

"This is fifty-one. I'm already on the scene," he yelled into the receiver. "Confirm—1121 Mockingbird Lane?"

"That's affirmative," dispatch responded.

Aaron felt the familiar rush of adrenaline fill his body. "Fifty-one responding. Request fifty-four stay en route."

"Fifty-four en route." The voice he recognized as Officer Adam Meuller's responded.

Aaron pulled his pistol from his holster and ducked into the night. He skirted the blue glow from the single streetlamp that lit the eastern side of the house, and flattened himself against the exterior stairwell to Katherine's apartment.

It had to be a ploy. He'd been watching the entrance to her house all night. Still, his heart was beating a fast cadence against his chest, and every cop's instinct he possessed was firing bullets at him. He wasn't about to let his guard down, whether the enemy was for real—or whether the enemy was Katherine.

He ascended the stairs, his back against the old wooden siding of the house. The grating of the soles of his running shoes against the concrete stairs irritated him, sounded unnatural against the backdrop of familiar night noises. How many damned stairs were there, anyway?

He reached the top and carefully tried the doorknob. It was locked. He'd failed to bring his flashlight, but everything appeared still and quiet as he risked a quick glance through the glass panes of the old wooden door. Too quiet. The only noise that disturbed the night was the gentle hum of the air-conditioning unit below the stairs.

He rapped his knuckles against the door. "Police," he called. "Open up."

He was met with a woman's scream—Katherine's scream. His blood froze in his veins for a brief moment before moving again, pushing him into action.

Aaron broke the glass pane with the butt of his pistol. He reached in through the jagged opening, turning the interior doorknob and letting himself in, a sharp slice to his wrist barely registering through the second rush of adrenaline. "Police!" He paused. "Katherine?" he called into the now-silent apartment.

"Help!" The frantic cry echoed toward him from the interior.

He switched on the overhead light, illuminating a small kitchen and a long hallway. "Katherine, where are you?"

"Here." The voice was calmer now, but weak. He'd heard the tone a hundred times before. Just before victims slipped into shock.

He glanced down the hallway, wondering which of the interior doors Katherine's voice was coming from and what condition he'd find her in. Before he could move, a resounding thud echoed from below. The sound of a door slamming. He froze, torn between the fear in Katherine's voice and the noise. "It's Detective Stone," he called. "Are you okay?"

"Yes." Her voice was breathless this time, as if she were afraid of being heard. "Did you hear that? He's downstairs."

Aaron whirled in place, looking for a stairwell. It was dawning on him now. Katherine's apartment wasn't separate from the rest of the house, but connected by an interior stairwell. Dammit, he'd been watching the wrong entrance. "Stay put!" he yelled. "I'll be back."

He flung open a door, but found himself face-to-face with neatly stacked linens and a vacuum cleaner. He ground his teeth together to keep from cursing and tried a second one. This time he was met by the dark void of a stairwell and a waft of cool air.

He grasped a wooden railing and flung himself recklessly down the stairs before hesitating at the bottom. What was wrong with him? He'd headed down the stairs like a bull in a china shop. No, worse, like a first-year rookie.

He pulled up short at a closed door at the bottom of the stairwell, bracing himself for whatever he might face on the other side. "Police!" he shouted before turning the knob and kicking the door open.

He stared down the barrel of his pistol into the dimly lit, neatly furnished, but empty duplex. An exterior door stood open on the far side of a small living room, squeaking slightly as the night air drifted inside.

Aaron found a light switch next to him and flipped it, illuminating most of the downstairs quarters with the action. He walked cautiously toward the open door, but knew he'd lost his chance. Sure enough, the only sound that accompanied the low hum of the air-conditioning unit was the steady chirping of katydids. He locked the door and did a brief inspection of the apartment. Nothing.

Katherine. It was as if someone whispered the word into his ear.

"No!" It was her voice. The word came from above him, terrified, outraged.

Aaron took the stairs two at a time, flinging open the upstairs door to Katherine's apartment. He ran down the hallway, toward the only open door. He reached what had to be her bedroom, fully lit but completely empty.

A nauseating feeling crept into his stomach. He glanced at the tangled disarray of sheets and quilt, at an overturned potted plant spilling its dirt onto the floor. "Katherine! Dammit, where are you?"

He cocked his head, listening. A voice, low and murmuring, was coming from the other end of the apartment. He hesitated, drawing in, determining everything he could from what he heard. The voice was female—Katherine's—and the conversation was soothing, like one you'd have with an injured child.

"Katherine?" he called.

"Here." Her answer was distracted, the single word spoken with what almost sounded like irritation. "I'm okay," she added.

A metal popping sound punctuated the silence that followed, and he headed toward the other end of the apartment at a jog, absently noticing the flashing blue lights that penetrated the sheer curtains of her kitchen. "It's about time, Meuller," he grumbled. He stepped over the broken glass that was scattered across the kitchen floor and opened the exterior door. Adam Meuller was just stepping from the squad car below.

"Meuller," he shouted, "everything's okay up here. Check the grounds." Adam waved to signal he'd understood.

Aaron turned back toward the kitchen and faced a solitary door. He hadn't noticed the door when he'd first entered the apartment. It probably led to a separate dining room, but it certainly would lead him to Katherine, and to the answer to this riddle.

He pushed open the door and froze.

Katherine was sitting on the floor of an empty dining room, her dog cradled in her arms. Scissors in hand, she was trying to clip away a thick mass of duct tape that was wrapped tightly around the dog's muzzle. Tears fell in a steady, silent stream, dropping onto her bare knees.

Aaron ran his hand through his hair, not knowing what to do. The little dog should be struggling, but wasn't. He looked at the duct tape that bound its stubby legs, hoping that was the reason. But he suspected there was more to it than that.

"He—he can't . . ." Katherine made cooing sounds to the dog as she tried in vain to ease the scissors between the dog's muzzle and the tape. "He can't breathe!" she finished, slamming the scissors against the floor in frustration. She looked up at Aaron, tears sliding across her cheeks and landing on her dust-streaked white T-shirt.

Aaron knelt next to her and turned her toward him. "We'll take care of him, but you first. Are you okay?"

She nodded. "I'm fine." She turned her attention back to the dog, lifting the scissors for a second try at the tape. She clipped at the edges without success. "He didn't—" she tried to continue. "What I mean is he never got close enough for me to even see him. Damn this tape. He can't breathe!"

Aaron lifted the dog's head. His breathing was labored, wheezing in and out in more of a rattled snore than a breath. "Do you have a shrimp knife?" Aaron asked.

Katherine nodded absently. "In the kitchen." Her eyes lit with understanding. "I'll get it."

Aaron took the dog in his arms, surprised at the heaviness of its limp body. He'd just settled the dachshund's long muzzle against the crook of his right arm when Katherine returned.

She squatted down next to him, and the essence of her played against his face, his senses. The soft honeysuckle scent of shampoo mixed with the musk of her skin. He watched her gentle determination as she lifted the dog's muzzle and tried to angle the shrimp knife beneath the tape without hurting the animal. She wasn't crying anymore, Aaron noted, and felt a surge of satisfaction that he'd helped.

It was at that moment that she changed, transformed before his eyes. His jaw clenched, the only outward sign of the battle between logic and instinct that warred within him. He slid the slender shrimp knife from her trembling fingers and tried to ignore the rush of male awareness at the touch of her warm skin against his. He didn't understand it, but he knew it without doubt: She hadn't killed Owen Blake.

He aimed the sharp point of the knife between the dog's eyes and wedged it as carefully between flesh and tape as possible, working in an easy back and forth motion until the knife reached the end of the dog's long muzzle. Turning the needle-sharp point upward, he ripped through the thick duct tape in one motion.

He held the dog tight as it squirmed. At least it was alive. "This is the hard part, buddy," he whispered.

He looked at Katherine, but she was already in motion. She grasped the edges of the severed duct tape and pulled downward, ripping it, along with a generous amount of fur, from the dog's muzzle.

The old dog gave a painful, weak yip. "I'm sorry, sweetie," Katherine murmured as the dog began to cough, sputtering and eventually gagging in his effort to swallow and breathe at the same time. Katherine had his legs unbound in a flash, and balled and threw the mass of duct tape angrily against the wall.

She removed the squirming dachshund from Aaron's arms and cuddled him like a baby. Tears spilled across her cheeks again, tears of relief, he thought.

"I couldn't lose you," she whispered against the dog's long ear as she rocked him back and forth. He nuzzled against her face in return.

She turned toward Aaron, fingers pressed against her full lips. He recognized the gesture, knew she was holding a flood of emotions in check. "Thank you," she whispered.

He ached to hold her. He wanted to pull her body against his, feel the soft, womanly roundness of her breasts pressed against his chest, brush the tears from her cheeks.

He lifted his hand to her arm, but the hurried sound of boots against concrete halted that action, and he ended up brushing a dusty cobweb from the sleeve of her T-shirt instead.

A heavy rap sounded against the kitchen door.

It would be Adam Meuller, Aaron thought, and illogically resented the interruption.

He looked at Katherine. Her long, heavy hair was pulled atop her head in a haphazard ponytail, but it still spilled easily past her shoulders. He thought back to the first time he'd seen her in the convertible, and the second time at the Herb Shop. Both times her hair had been contained in some way. Suddenly he wanted to see it down, wanted to see it swinging against the curve of her hips.

His hand drifted toward her against his will. His fingers found the sleeve of her shirt and trailed upward—against the delicate skin of her upper arm, across the warm cotton that covered her shoulder, eventually hesitating in the curve of her neck. He allowed his fingers to caress the silky flesh he found there, and beneath his fingers her pulse quickened.

A second rap sounded against the door.

Aaron caught himself, and clasped Katherine's shoulder in what he hoped was a concerned, yet official gesture. "That's one of our officers. Are you going to be okay for a minute?"

She glanced down at his hand for the briefest of moments before meeting his eyes. "Yes."

He went back into the kitchen, stepping over fragments of glass to open the damaged door. A breathless Meuller waited on the other side. As Aaron had suspected, the other officer's search hadn't turned up anything. Aaron filled Meuller in on the details of the call, and promised to wrap things up himself. He had a hunch Meuller would be eager to let him complete the paperwork. He was right.

What disturbed Aaron was his own eagerness to get back to Katherine. Before he'd even closed the door behind Meuller, she entered the kitchen, still holding the dog and still looking like she needed holding herself.

He had no business thinking like that. He rolled the tight muscles of his shoulders, determined to shake off the rush of desire he felt. Hell, all she'd done was walk in the room, and he'd felt the heat.

He fixed his gaze on the dachshund. "Do you think he needs to see a vet?"

She stroked the top of the dog's head so hard, Aaron thought its round eyes were going to pop out. She glanced at the glowing digital clock of the microwave. "It's two o'clock in the morning."

He couldn't tell if the sentence was a statement or a question.

"Dr. Blankenship is elderly," she continued. "I hate to wake him at this hour." She shifted the dog's weight in her arms. "I really don't think there's anything he could do for him that I can't do here at home. I think he just needs some rest and some TLC. I'll take him first thing in the morning."

Aaron nodded, then glanced around at the pine cabinets that lined the small kitchen. "Where do you keep your cereal bowls?" he asked. "I'll get him some water."

Her answering smile was weak, but the light in her eyes told him he'd said something right. "Just to the right of the sink," she answered. "Thanks."

He filled a small glass bowl with cool water and set it on the kitchen floor. At first he thought it was going to take a crowbar to loosen Katherine's grip on the dog, but eventually she sat him on the floor beside the bowl. The dog tilted his gray muzzle at first, eyeing the water suspiciously before he began to lap it up. Before long, he toddled off into the adjacent living room and curled up with a satisfied sigh on a sheepskin rug beside the sofa.

Katherine chuckled. "Meet Roscoe. He owns the place."

Aaron couldn't help but smile too. Until he looked at Katherine. She was standing with her back to him, her slender fingers curled over the edge of the kitchen countertop, a simple silver ring adorning her right hand. Her white T-shirt was wrinkled and dotted with dust below the trail of her long hair. He absently wondered how she'd gotten so dirty—until his gaze slid across her hips and down her bare legs.

Then all rational thought left him entirely. The T-shirt barely skimmed the tops of her thighs, and Aaron found himself wondering what she wore beneath the simple fabric, if her legs were as silky soft as they looked . . .

She turned toward him at that moment, saving him from his own traitorous thoughts. But her expression was a mixture of surprise and embarrassment, and Aaron knew she sensed the lust that was pounding through his veins. Never mind that she was still a suspect. At the moment he was more ashamed of taking advantage of the situation—or at least of wanting to.

She rubbed her hands against her upper arms, and he noticed she was trembling. Her gaze flicked to his before darting back to the floor. "I should get my robe."

She disappeared down the long hall before he could form a response. It was just as well. He didn't know how to explain to himself the raw hunger she must have seen in his eyes, much less explain it to her.

He paced the small kitchen, uncertain what to do with himself, or with the irrational attraction he felt for

Katherine. He tried to focus on the elation he'd experienced at the Scenic View Inn when he'd first traced the call to her. Nothing. It was crazy, but he felt nothing except a sense of denial on her behalf.

I couldn't stay . . . He was too young for me. An old, familiar surge of anger twisted his gut. He summoned it. It was just what he needed to put things back into perspective.

Maybe, just maybe he could have believed she'd called the hotel because of some weird dream. But she'd taken the ruse too far. No, she hadn't thought he'd buy her psychic, mumbo-jumbo story. She'd thought to scare him away from the investigation by proving she had contacts in the department.

Aaron shook his head. That she knew someone in the force was the only logical explanation. And she'd used that connection to poke her nose where it didn't belong—in his past. But hell, everybody knew his story. He could picture any number of cops willing to share their secrets, and his, with a woman who looked like Katherine.

He felt his anger melting into weariness, and hated himself for it. He hated weakness, especially his own. Ten years ago he'd let the sadness weigh him down, practically suck the life from him. He ran his hand through his hair as he paced. It had been hard enough to put Jacqueline's death in the past without someone stirring around in it—throwing his failure back into his face. Back into his dreams.

He stopped pacing. No, Jacqueline had haunted his dreams last night, hours before he'd ever laid eyes on Katherine Jackson. It was the same dream he'd dreamed a thousand times. In it he begged her to stay, but she wouldn't.

I couldn't stay . . . He was too young for me. Katherine's voice taunted him again.

Was it possible Katherine had dreamed . . . He tried the idea on for size, then shook his head. *You're losing it, Stone,* he told himself. Katherine had likely bought his story for the price of a beer and an hour or two of her time at Kelley's bar, the local cop hangout.

But she couldn't have. Aaron began pacing again, trying to think. Had she had time? He rubbed his eyes. Between the stakeout at the Scenic View Inn the night before and pulling an all-nighter this night, his days and nights were running together. He'd only approached Katherine today—no, that was actually yesterday. Which meant—

He felt her return before he heard her. She walked softly, barefoot, down the hardwood floor of the hallway, still fastening the belt of a terry-and-silk robe. He noticed a frustrated set to her features and, as she neared, saw that her fingers were shaking uncontrollably.

She looked up, an apologetic, embarrassed expression on her face, and clasped her hands together. "Delayed reaction, I suppose," she said.

He watched the single knot of the belt loosen and separate. He didn't doubt that the trembling was an honest reaction to fear, and he didn't doubt that the break-in was for real. But he should have. He felt the muscles of his shoulders stiffen. He should be questioning everything about this woman.

He crossed the distance between them and retied

the belt, forcing his fingers to complete the task without touching her, without straying from the soft fabric. But he couldn't stop the womanly scent of her skin from surrounding him, couldn't stop his mind from calculating her height against his own, wondering where their bodies would meet if he held her.

Satisfied that his hands, if not his mind, had cooperated, he stepped back and met her eyes. She clasped her fingers beneath her chin. "Thank you." The words were almost a whisper.

It was then that Aaron noticed the blue-green mark that circled her wrist. Without thinking, he reached out for her, rubbing his thumb over the bruise. "Did this happen tonight?" Anger drummed through his veins. "I thought you said he didn't touch you."

"He didn't," she said, pulling her arm from his grasp.

He turned her by the shoulder. "Then what—"

"You did it."

The words were simple. Not an accusation, but a statement. He'd done it? His mind buzzed, searching for the answer. Of course. Guilt stabbed at him as he recalled the ugly scene in front of the Herb Shop.

He was overwhelmed by the urge to make things better—overwhelmed by her. "I'm so sorry." The words hung between them for a moment, but only for a moment.

His hands found her shoulders, and his palms molded the soft material of her robe. Then she was against him, her body pressed so tightly to his that he could feel her heartbeat. He allowed one hand to slide between her shoulder blades, press her closer, so close that he felt the hardening of her nipples beneath the fabric.

She was trembling. He knew that fact was going to leave him aching with need . . . and save him from making a mistake. He shifted his hips away from her body, hoping she hadn't felt his immediate arousal, and forced his expression to appear casual.

"Are you okay now?" He smiled down into her face, praying he was a good enough actor to pull off the charade. "You looked like you needed a hug." He dropped his hands from her shoulders and nonchalantly guided her toward the sofa. "Victims often have delayed reactions to stress. Can I fix you something to drink? It might help you relax."

She sat down on the sofa and nodded. "I don't drink, but I think I might try a cup of chamomile tea."

When she started to rise, he stopped her. "No, let me. Just tell me where you keep it."

She gestured toward the kitchen. "In the cabinet above the stove."

Aaron was relieved to have something to do. He made his way back into the kitchen and swung open the cabinet door. At least fifteen boxes of chamomile tea were stacked neatly in the small cabinet. He looked at Katherine over his shoulder. "I take it you like chamomile tea?"

An unsure smile played across her face before she answered. "Actually, no, I don't. But Grams—she's my . . . Well, she used to be my foster mother. Anyway, she thinks it's good for my insomnia." Katherine shrugged. "I don't have the heart to tell her that I hate it, and she keeps replenishing my stock."

Aaron raised one eyebrow in question. "I have a thermos of coffee in the car if you'd like some instead."

He thought she was about to say yes until she looked down at her hands again. "No, thanks. I think I'll try the chamomile tonight after all."

Aaron filled a coffee mug with hot water and added a tea bag of what looked and smelled like grass clippings. Glancing at Katherine, he found her watching him intently from the sofa in the adjoining room, her hands again clasped beneath her chin. He set the mug in the microwave and punched the minute button.

Drumming his fingers against the countertop, he tried not to think about temptation—tried not to think about the woman in the other room who looked and behaved like anything except a suspect in a murder case. How long could one minute drag on, anyway? He glanced at the broken pane in the kitchen door.

A tiny moth fluttered in on the night breeze that flowed through the jagged opening, and began to circle the incandescent light overhead, reminding him that Katherine's apartment was no longer secure. He rubbed his thumb over the shallow cut that trailed across his left wrist. He actually felt guilty that he'd shattered the windowpane, leaving the apartment—and Katherine—vulnerable.

The microwave's buzzer sounded, and he removed the cup of tea, thinking that the steam that rose from it smelled only slightly nauseating.

"Thank you," Katherine said as he handed her the mug.

Aaron thought she still looked faint, but forced

himself to look away, to get on with the business at hand. "I need to ask you a few questions."

She cradled the thick stoneware mug between her palms and nodded. "I'd almost forgotten that you would need to fill out a report." She stole a quick glance at the sleeping dog before meeting Aaron's eyes.

He'd forgotten, too, Aaron thought. "The questions will only relate to what happened here tonight. Do you understand?"

"You're telling me I don't need to call my lawyer. Not yet, anyway. Is that right?"

Aaron sighed, suddenly feeling the lateness of the hour, and resenting like hell the attraction he felt for the woman who was looking at him with the most beautiful, most accusing eyes he'd ever seen. "I'm trying to tell you that you don't need to be concerned about this line of questioning. I only need to complete a report on the break-in."

She took a hesitant sip of tea, looking away from him.

He decided her silence was probably as close to a yes as he was going to get. "I'll just be a minute," he said, heading toward the door.

"Where are you going?" Behind him, Katherine shifted on the sofa, the alarm in her voice obvious despite the neutral expression on her face.

"I need to get the forms from the car," he answered.

He followed her gaze to the glass-littered kitchen floor, then to the useless fragments of the pane that remained in the door.

And he saw, through her eyes, the darkness that loomed just beyond the single streetlight.

Dammit. He glanced at his watch. The horizon would be streaked with the glow of morning in a couple of hours. Katherine would feel safer then.

He walked out the door, closing it behind him as he stepped into the darkness. He welcomed the damp night air that clung to his face and arms, clearing his thoughts. What the hell had just happened in there?

He descended the stairs two at a time, crossed the dew-streaked grass to his car, threw open the car door, and snatched up the radio receiver. "Car fifty-one to dispatch."

"Dispatch to fifty-one."

"Jacobs is working Roadie's tonight." Aaron slammed the heavy car door shut behind him, blocking the increasing number of bugs that were buzzing about the interior light. "See if he's available to pull surveillance at 1121 Mockingbird." He paused, then hit the talk button again. "I'll authorize," he added.

And take the heat.

He leaned his head back against the seat, thinking that comfort was really relevant to how tired you were.

Static crackled over the radio, and Aaron sat up. "Dispatch to fifty-one. Negative on Jacobs. He's not responding."

"Roger, dispatch," he answered. He let the button of the receiver snap back into position. "Dammit!" he shouted. Just his luck. He depressed the receiver's button again. "Fifty-one out of service."

He filled out everything he could in the solitude of the car before making the now-familiar trek back across the yard and up the stairs to Katherine's apartment. He almost knocked on the door, but peered through the glass instead. He could see beyond the small kitchen and into the shadows of the living room, where Katherine was curled against the brightly colored cushions of her sofa. Her relaxed posture warned him that she was asleep.

He eased the door open and crossed the small kitchen to the sofa. It was then he noticed she had pulled the dog onto her lap, her long fingers wrapped possessively around his body. The dachshund lifted his graying muzzle, examined Aaron thoughtfully, then nestled back against Katherine.

Aaron glanced around the rambling old duplex, taking in the rough country antiques that were placed in various corners, the jungle of houseplants that crowded countertops and windowsills. His gaze moved to the now-empty mug that rested on a coaster in the center of her coffee table.

He'd spent ten years on the force, and listening to his own intuition had gotten him this far—not to mention saving his butt a couple hundred times. Something wasn't right. Despite evidence to the contrary, Katherine Jackson was about as far from the typical murder suspect as you could get. Aaron allowed his gaze to fall on her face, noticing the way her long lashes rested against her cheeks, the unpretentious tangle of dark hair that fell across her shoulders.

He plopped down in the most uncomfortable wicker chair he'd ever had the displeasure of coming in contact with, and watched Katherine as she slept. Her breathing was shallow, but moved the silk-and-terry material against her throat in a hypnotic rhythm. She started once, and her fingers stroked the dog in her lap before her breathing returned to normal.

Logic would have him believe the woman before him was a murderer, yet every male instinct he possessed just wanted to get closer. Aaron gripped the stiff wicker arms of the chair and forced his body to relax.

He had to get some rest. He had a murder to solve, and his current suspect wasn't working out.

FOUR

Katherine stretched her arms in front of her, flexing her fingers and working the stiff muscles of her shoulders. Moaning, she pressed her cheek into her pillow. Then she felt him, felt the intensity of his gaze against her body as surely as she felt the morning sunlight slanting through the window.

She opened her eyes. He was sprawled in the small wicker chair, his masculine body covering the feminine piece of furniture in fascinating contrast. His arms were draped over the sides, one hand holding her cordless phone, the other drooping almost to the floor. His body was relaxed, but his eyes were alert. And he was watching her.

It all came rushing back to her—the break-in, Roscoe, the dizzy panic she'd experienced in Aaron's arms. But the fear she'd felt the night before was gone. Maybe it was the lingering lethargy of sleep, or maybe it was simply the fact that she was safe, protected.

Whatever it was had nothing to do with the dangerous look in Detective Aaron Stone's eyes.

Suddenly she wanted to know, felt she had to ask the one question that illogically hadn't occurred to her until then. She squeezed the pillow beneath her cheek for reassurance.

"How was Owen Blake killed?" The question sounded stark, the echo of her voice only remotely connected to her body.

He didn't seem the least bit surprised. "That's not something we should discuss without your lawyer present." He set the phone on the floor and pulled his legs to him with a lazy stretch. "In fact, that's not something I should discuss with you at all."

There was a finality in his answer, but somehow Katherine knew he'd tell her. If she was bold enough to ask again. She closed her eyes and remained still. She didn't want to risk breaking the strange bond, the spell that surrounded them in the quiet stillness of the apartment. She could feel the connection, the suspicion, the hostility. . . .

She opened her eyes and met his steel-blue gaze. She could feel the attraction.

"Tell me anyway," she whispered. "How was he killed?"

His gaze flicked over her body, his eyes narrowing when they finally met hers. "A thirty-eight was placed against the side of his head, a pillow over his face." The corners of his mouth lifted, but it wasn't exactly a smile. "Boom. You know the rest."

She couldn't help but wince at the image, but she

knew when she was being baited. She sat up, smoothing the wrinkles from her robe as if it mattered.

"No, I don't. But I have a pretty good idea."

He shrugged. "You asked."

"Why?"

"Why what?"

"What was the motive?"

Aaron looked at her suspiciously for a moment, then stood and paced in front of the sofa. "Okay. I'll bite."

"What—?"

He cleared his throat and began to speak, his words sounding more like monotone dictation than an answer. "The victim was found facedown on the floor in room 315 of the Scenic View Inn. A small quantity of cocaine was found in proximity to the body. The victim died from a close-range gunshot wound to the head. It is believed that the murder was drug-related, but no hard evidence has been found."

He stopped directly in front of her and placed his hands on his hips before continuing. "However, someone did attempt to contact the deceased. Luckily the call was traced—"

Katherine stood, her body brushing against his before he took a surprised step backward. "The call was traced to one Katherine Jackson of 1121 Mockingbird Lane," she finished. "Yet the suspect appears to have no motive for the crime."

He closed the slight distance between them, and she felt her bravado falter as he looked into her eyes. Dark lashes rimmed his, making their light blue color startlingly vivid. They could be cold as ice. Or, she realized, a gray-blue that smoldered with emotion.

"Even more curious," he continued, "the suspect's residence was burglarized. . . ."

"Tell me something, Detective." Katherine mocked his posture by placing her hands on her hips. "If the motive of the crime was drug-related, why was the cocaine left behind?"

A dark look of suspicion and—could it be respect?—crossed his face. He raised his hand and brushed her cheek with his knuckles. Warm, rough, seductive. A man's touch. How long had it been since she'd been touched that way? Something inside her—something hard and wary—melted with the simple contact of skin against skin. Yet with it came a strange sense of confidence. He wanted to touch her.

A woman's power over a man.

Abruptly he dropped his hand and stepped away, turning his back to her. "Someone from Graves' Glass Repair will be by to replace the windowpane."

"That's not necessary. I can—"

"Two things: Don't answer the door for anyone else, and don't leave town."

As he walked through the kitchen, Katherine noticed that the broken glass had vanished from the floor.

He turned back toward her. "The first is a suggestion. The second is an order."

She felt a now-familiar surge of anger twist in her stomach. It was too early, and she was still too shaken by last night to tolerate his macho crap. She smiled sweetly and watched his expression go from commanding to confused. It was the same expression she'd seen on his face in her dream . . . when she'd asked him his name.

Then instinctively she knew, and she also knew that the knowledge would unsettle him. The temptation was too sweet to resist.

"One other thing, Detective."

His eyes narrowed again. "What is it?"

"Do you resemble Owen Blake?"

The question got a hearty laugh from him. He opened the door and pressed his hip against it. "That's difficult to say, considering half his face was gone."

She struggled to keep her expression neutral, to keep the upper hand. "Never mind."

"Okay." He ran his hand through his hair, and the dark waves fell back into place with maddening perfection. "No. He was short, balding, ten, maybe fifteen years my senior. Why?"

"Well now I really am confused," she stated with the same sweet smile she'd fabricated earlier. "I was so certain that you were planning to pose as Owen Blake—go undercover." She waved her hand. "Whatever the official term for it is."

"No, sorry to disappoint you. Not unless you count being a nasty surprise on the other side of a hotel door or a voice over the phone." He shrugged, a sarcastic smile playing about his lips as he stepped outside. "But you didn't want to talk to me—or rather to Owen Blake. Remember?"

"I remember." She caught the door as he tried to close it. "So you were ready to pose as Owen Blake if I had asked to be put through. . . ." She nodded. "Now it makes perfect sense."

He looked at her, his eyes distrustful. "It does, does it?"

"Yes." She pulled the ponytail holder from her hair, then shook her hair out. Casually, she caught the long mane and replaced the thick band with a satisfied snap. "The man in my dream was you."

This time his expression went from wary to downright amused. She could tell he was struggling to maintain his usual poker face.

"In my dream I asked you your name," she finished. "I didn't understand your answer until now."

"Because?"

"Because you told me it was Owen Blake."

She closed the door behind him before he could respond, and pushed the dead bolt into place, punctuating her dismissal of him. Through the glass she caught the surprise on his face, the flash of possibility, before it was replaced by another cynical shake of his head.

She watched him as he descended the stairs and made his way to the unmarked car that waited on the other side of the street. It was then she realized that Aaron had answered the 911 call before the uniformed officer had. He'd been watching her.

She rubbed frantically at the chill bumps that flowed across her upper arms, then looked down at the jagged glass that still remained in the diamond-shaped door pane. Was it standard procedure to repair damage? She doubted it, and that meant she'd have to be in touch to repay the cost.

And she had a feeling that owing Aaron Stone would cost her far more than she was willing to pay.

"There's nothing in the background check that would lead us to believe she had anything to do with the murder."

Aaron leaned across the desk, scanning the report. "So how do you explain the telephone call?"

Lieutenant Dawson tossed his reading glasses onto his desk and rubbed his wrinkled forehead. "I've given you a wide berth on this one, Aaron. I expect *you* to tell *me* that."

He'd slept away most of the previous day after leaving Katherine's apartment. Then he'd prowled around his house half the night, going over case notes, considering possibilities he had no right to consider. He'd even gotten in his truck and driven down Mockingbird Lane to make certain a squad car was still pulling surveillance. It had been.

Lieutenant Dawson retrieved his glasses and tucked them into the front pocket of his shirt. "She should have been brought in for questioning right away. You know that, don't you?"

Aaron turned to stare through the glass that separated the lieutenant's office from the larger outer office, which was buzzing with activity. "Maybe."

"And as hesitant as I was to authorize it, you shouldn't have blown surveillance."

He met the older man's gaze. "She was in danger."

"Was she?"

Aaron turned away again. Yes, she'd actually been in danger. He knew it. He couldn't prove it, but it was a fact. Unfortunately, answers like that didn't translate very well when it came to the lieutenant. Dawson was rational, logical, unswayed by the emotions that made good cops better, mediocre cops dead.

Lieutenant Dawson took a swig of coffee and leveled a commanding stare in Aaron's direction. "Have you advised her that she's not to leave town?"

He nodded.

"Good. Because I'm afraid I can't authorize any more surveillance unless additional evidence is found."

Aaron felt a ripple of tension settle in his shoulders. He'd been expecting it. Funny, though, it felt more like a reprimand for the way he'd handled the case than a routine decision. But he knew better. The lieutenant was nothing if not fair.

Aaron leaned his head toward his right shoulder, stretching the stiff muscles of his neck. The lieutenant would have his badge on a peg if he knew he'd stayed the night at Katherine's, if he knew the information he'd shared with her the next morning.

Damn, but he'd been reckless with this case.

"Any objection to my keeping an eye on her myself?" Aaron kept his back turned to the older man.

He could hear the rustle of paper behind him, then a deep sigh. "No. Not other than the fact that one of my detectives on a murder case thinks that, unlike the rest of us mortals, he doesn't need sleep."

Aaron turned to smile in the lieutenant's direction, knowing he'd won the battle if not the war. But another question flitted through his mind—did he want to keep Katherine under surveillance or protect her? He ignored that question.

"You know what they say. Shoot a cop and he'll bleed coffee."

"Well, try not to find out until I retire." Dawson strained to look over Aaron's shoulder, and Aaron pivoted to find Johnny Jacobs pacing in front of the door. "What the hell does he want now?" The lieutenant shook his head. "Every time I turn around that kid is in my office."

Aaron seized the distraction to open the door. It was the perfect opportunity to escape the list of dos and don'ts that he knew was about to be tossed in his direction. The lieutenant was from the old school, and he had definitely skipped the class on bending the rules.

"Jacobs." Aaron motioned for the rookie to enter as he eased out the door. "We're all done here."

"Just a minute, Stone—" Dawson started to rise.

"I'll give you a call," Aaron said over his shoulder, already halfway across the busy outer office.

He'd be in hot water if the lieutenant ever found out he'd told Katherine the details of the case. He recalled the soft furrow of worry between her eyes as she'd asked him about Owen Blake's murder. His hand had ached to smooth away her anxiety, and his lips had ached to taste the skin of her cheek, explore the hollow of her bare neck. . . . But he'd spilled his guts instead.

He shook his head in self-disgust. Pillow talk was supposed to be a hell of a lot more fun, wasn't it?

Katherine opened the cabinet door and stared at the boxes of chamomile tea. Letting the cabinet door close with a thud, she turned to the refrigerator for a cola instead. Roscoe padded into the kitchen to stare at her as she popped the top.

She pulled the sash of her robe tighter, looking down into the questioning face of her best friend. "Get off my case. What, the sugar and caffeine are going to keep me up?" She threw her hands in the air, laughing. "Believe me, I'm already awake."

She sipped the soda, then crossed to the window. Moving the sheer curtains to one side, she tapped absently on the pane with short-clipped fingernails. "I can't sleep when someone's *not* watching me." The dark veil of night prevented her from seeing through the window of the beige sedan parked across the street, but she didn't have to.

Then an idea occurred to her. And why not? She was tired of feeling like a bug under glass. On impulse she grabbed a second cola and threw open the kitchen door. She would have felt exposed, vulnerable, walking down the stairs and across the moonlit courtyard to the car that waited on the other side—if she hadn't been certain that she was safe. Safe because of the man who was, no doubt, watching her from the car.

It was easier to look down, to watch the soft imprint her bare feet made in the dew-laden Bermuda grass than it was to look up at the car. But eventually, as she stepped onto the warm pavement of the road, she had to.

His window was rolled down, and one arm, tan and bare below the sleeve of a black T-shirt, was resting against the door of the sedan. The look in his eyes was deadly.

"What the hell do you think you're doing?" He fired the question at her.

Katherine squared her shoulders, welcoming the fight. Anything was better than pacing her apartment.

She extended the soda. "I thought you might like something cold to drink—since you don't appear to be going anywhere."

"What are you doing up at this time of night?"

"It's morning," she corrected him. "And unfortunately I'm awake often at this time of day." She met his questioning stare. "Last time I checked, insomnia wasn't an illegal activity."

His eyes softened slightly, but his right hand tightened around the steering wheel.

When he didn't respond, she continued. "Maybe I don't understand how this works. What good does it do to watch someone when they know they're being watched?"

This time Aaron laughed. "You weren't supposed to know."

Katherine found herself smiling with him. "Well, the car is a little obvious. No one in their right mind would drive a car this ugly unless it was issued to them."

"Well, unfortunately the police department doesn't authorize antique sports cars." He finally pulled the can from her hand and cocked an eyebrow. "Most store clerks can't afford them, either."

"It was Mike's." She hesitated when she caught a flash of emotion in his eyes. My God, it looked like jealousy. No, surely she was mistaken. "Mike is my foster parents' son," she continued. "He left the car behind when he joined the air force. It was a wreck of an old thing." She smiled, recalling the shape the Cutlass had been in before she'd had it restored. "I rescued it."

His gaze flickered over her body, and for a moment she thought she saw lust behind his eyes. Then it was gone, and he threw back the soda, drinking at least half the can. "She's a beauty," he said.

"I have the before and after pictures if you'd like to come up and see them." The words were out before she realized what she'd said, what she'd offered.

Aaron looked surprised as well. "Better not. It's against the rules, you know."

That was laughable since he didn't strike her as the type to follow the rules. "I thought the rule was to not be seen in the first place."

He drank the last of the soda, bent the can, and sat the empty aluminum shell on the passenger's seat. "Score one for the psychic."

Katherine shot him an evil look before she recognized the humor in his expression. "Well, at the rate of speed you drank that, you'll want to use my bathroom soon anyway."

He nodded and opened the car door. "Besides, you'd like the chance to prove that you're not a murderer. Right?"

"Score one for the detective."

Katherine suddenly found herself nervous as Aaron unfolded his body from the car. Searching for something to say, she focused on the holster strapped to the outside of his black T-shirt, which was stretched distractingly tight across his chest.

"I'll bet your badge would be on a peg if it got around that you'd turned down the chance to prowl around my apartment without a search warrant."

His badge on a peg . . . Aaron repeated silently. Hadn't he thought that same thing earlier that day? His first idea was that she'd spent time around cops, but the phrase was one his first partner had used, and Aaron had picked it up from him. His first partner wasn't only retired, he'd been dead for several years.

Aaron rubbed his right temple. For the life of him, he couldn't think of anyone else on the force who used the phrase. He looked up to judge her reaction as he spoke. "Yeah, you're right. My badge would be on a peg."

She didn't react at all. In fact, she just turned and started walking toward the duplex. Aaron shook his head, shook off the ludicrous idea that she'd read his mind, then followed her toward the house.

The structure was simple—painted white siding with traditional black shutters, neatly trimmed boxwoods and azaleas lining the foundation. Katherine was barefoot, he noticed, wearing the same robe she'd changed into the night of the break-in. Her hair was pulled atop her head in that childlike ponytail again. Nothing about her was pretentious, yet everything about her was seductive in a natural, unassuming way.

He doubted that she intended to have this effect on him. Creamy white ankles flashed as she picked her way across the damp grass, and the sway of her hips was all but hidden beneath the silky robe. She tied him up inside—made him long for something he'd stopped longing for ten years ago.

His mind was turning over possibilities as he followed her through the door of her apartment, and not all of them were job related. As the door closed behind him, he was struck with a sense of déjà vu. He recalled the way Katherine's hands had trembled as she'd ripped the tape from the old dog's muzzle, her tears falling against the soft skin of her thigh. Then cruelly his mind replayed the rush of desire he'd felt as he'd finally held her against his body. . . .

"The bathroom is at the end of the hall. Adjaçent to the bedroom."

Her words stopped his flow of thought, and he was both irritated and grateful for the interruption. He looked up to find her smiling, but doubt as well as humor sparkled in her green eyes.

He decided not to tip the scales with a caustic remark. "Thanks."

The first thing he noticed as he entered her bedroom was that the potted plant had been lovingly tucked back into its nest of dirt and generously watered. Like a mother giving her child a glass of juice after a scraped knee, he thought.

The room was tidy but was liberally marked with Katherine's personality. A stack of romance novels sat atop a battered oak nightstand. Wooden blinds covered the windows, and numerous plants sat atop the windowsill. Tucked between a cactus and a trailing vine sat a smiling stone-carved cherub.

Good Lord, if she'd hired a decorator to convince him she wasn't a murderer, they couldn't have done a better job.

When he entered the bathroom, he decided that

there must be Gypsy blood running through her veins. The deep maroon stripes of the shower curtain should have clashed with the floral-patterned window curtain, but didn't. Yet another houseplant was crowded into the small room, this one hanging from a filigree plant hanger next to the window. A quick glance at its proximity to the toilet—and his shoulder—told him that Katherine didn't entertain men often.

Somehow that thought brightened him.

When he turned toward the sink, he noticed a number of photographs wedged between an oval mirror and its frame. Some of the pictures were old—one of an elderly couple standing in front of a 70s model Buick, a younger Katherine standing by a Grand Opening sign to the Herb Shop. Others were new—numerous photos of the dachshund, and two studio shots of three blond-headed children.

He turned on the cold water spigot and let the water pool in the palms of his hands. Operate on the facts, he reminded himself. Anything else was a recipe for disaster. He splashed the water on his face and blotted himself dry on a worn green hand towel.

As he passed through her bedroom and into the hallway, he hesitated. Katherine's bedroom was situated at the end of the hall, but two additional doors were accessible from it. He knew from the night of the break-in that one was a linen closet, but the other was a mystery. He glanced toward the kitchen. Katherine was standing on tiptoe, thoroughly engrossed in searching a top cabinet.

What the hell was he waiting for? Hadn't she practically invited him to inspect her apartment? If she was so determined to prove herself an unlikely suspect, he was more than willing to take her up on the offer. Only a small stab of guilt plagued him as he opened the second door and stepped inside.

Aaron flipped on the light switch, and waited while a fluorescent fixture flickered to illuminate the room in stark blue-white light. While Katherine's bedroom and bathroom had been filled with her personality, the second bedroom was almost sterile. A large room with a wide expanse of hardwood floor, it lacked warmth, to say the least. Inexpensive white blinds covered two floor-length windows, and the only item in the room was an ironing board placed diagonally in one corner, blocking yet another door.

Aaron's running shoes squeaked against the polished wood floor as he entered and crossed to the only thing of interest in the room—dual bifold doors that dominated one wall. The doors opened smoothly on their hinges, revealing the contents of the closet.

"Well I'll be damned," he muttered. "Cinderella goes to the ball."

The closet was jammed with dresses. Not the type of dresses that a store clerk wore to an herb shop, he thought cynically. There were at least thirty of the most ornate, no doubt expensive, evening gowns he'd ever seen. So exactly where did Katherine Jackson wear such creations? Tennessee offered plenty of opportunities for debutantes and families from old money. But orphaned store clerks? Not likely.

New money—dirty money—on the other hand, would offer a beautiful woman like Katherine plenty. He felt his shoulders stiffen at the thought of Katherine on the arm of some drug-running son of a bitch who was only interested in flaunting her beauty.

Someone who didn't know she tended houseplants and old dachshunds with the same loving care that some people had trouble giving their own children.

Anger twisted within him as he removed one of the gowns. Supple black velvet flowed beneath his fingers, topped by a cascade of creamy white satin that bordered a plunging neckline. Shining black beads formed a swirling pattern below the white satin, then parted to run the length of the velvet on each side of the gown.

He hung the dress back in the closet, blotting out the image of her wearing the beautiful gown—or any of the others that were hidden inside.

Aaron glanced over his shoulder. He didn't have long, but he had to know what was behind the other door. The ironing board had been too carefully placed in front of it, and experience had taught him that people hid only two things: things of value and things they were ashamed of. He was about to find out what Katherine Jackson didn't want anyone to see.

Squeezing between the window and the ironing board, he reached out to turn the doorknob.

"I don't want you to go in there." Katherine's voice was soft, her words more a request than an order.

He paused, then his hand dropped to his side as he turned to face her. She stood in the doorway to the near-empty room, still barefoot and still looking vulnerable.

"Why?" he asked. "What don't you want me to see?"

She crossed her arms and hugged them to her

chest. "There's nothing incriminating in there, if that's what you mean."

"You're the one who suggested I prowl around your apartment, remember?"

She raised her chin, and he recognized the determined look in her eyes. She was preparing for a fight. "Is it so surprising that I'd like to prove my innocence?"

"Then prove it."

"I've tried to. You don't believe me."

"Ah . . . the dream again."

"Yes, the dream again. I know you don't believe me, but calling the hotel was a lark. And now some weird coincidence has turned me into a murder suspect."

Aaron balled his fists, then forced himself to relax his hands. He had to admit that he hadn't considered her a true suspect since the night of the break-in. But she wasn't in the clear yet. Not by a long shot. "You do this—this psychic stuff, I mean?"

She looked away. "A little. Sometimes. By accident."

"Well, that'll stand up in court."

"Look, I've had some strange experiences in my life that can't be easily explained away, that's all." She shoved at a lock of hair that had escaped her ponytail. "It's not as if I know how to do it. It just happens when it happens."

"So that's supposed to explain why I can't go in this room?" He gestured toward the door.

"It's not a room. It's just a storage closet."

Aaron thought she looked tired, and for a moment

he was tempted to back off. But he couldn't. Not yet. He placed his hand on the doorknob. "Really?"

She crossed the room as silently as a cat. When she reached for the ironing board, he thought she would fling it aside. Instead she drew a deep breath, squared her shoulders, and lifted it carefully out of her way. She steadied the iron as it teetered, then turned to face him.

"Excuse me," she said too politely as she stepped up to the door.

He moved out of her way, sensing the swell of emotions that waited to burst through the wall of composure she'd built. She opened the door, flipped the light switch on the inside wall, then moved aside for him to enter.

He was dumbfounded, to say the least. The small walk-in closet was filled from floor to ceiling with fabric. Bolts of velvet and satin hung from wall hooks, yards of lace dripped from crude wooden shelves to pool against the bare floor. An old sewing machine sat in one corner, beside it a folded aluminum picnic table. Both were nearly hidden by some sort of shimmering net.

She wasn't Cinderella, Aaron thought. She was her own fairy godmother.

When he turned toward her, her eyes were filled with tears. Instinctively he knew he'd trodden on some personal, forbidden ground, stripped bare something that wished to remain cloaked in secrecy. And now there was nothing he could say, nothing he could do. Except take her hand and pull her into the room with him.

He heard her gasp as his fingers circled her wrist,

yet she followed without protest. Entering the small room was like entering another world. What had he expected—a stockpile of drugs, some secret command post for illegal activity? Instead he entered a fantasyland of mother-of-pearl sparkles and shimmering golden lace. The unique smell of freshly dyed cloth mixed with the mechanical scent of machine oil. Easter as a kid, he thought. Standing for what seemed like an eternity while his mother poked and prodded, pinned and hemmed.

Only Katherine probably hadn't shared that experience. He knew from the background check he'd run that she had been in the foster care system since she was nine. She hadn't had a mother to insist she stand still, to fuss over the details of some beloved Easter dress or silly Halloween costume.

He turned to face her, and his hand instantly reached out to stroke her cheek. "You made them?" he asked, wiping away a tear. "The gowns in the closet?"

"I—" She nodded.

"They're beautiful. You're beautiful."

"No, I'm not. I never have been." She looked away. "I was always too tall, too big and gangly."

"I don't know what you *were*, I only know what you are now." He allowed his gaze to flow over her body, the long legs, full hips, and large breasts, and finally the perfect ivory column of her neck. "I'm sure you have men falling over one another when you wear those dresses."

She pulled away from his touch and laughed. It was a deep, throaty laugh that had its own ring of cynicism to it. "I wouldn't know. I've never worn one outside this room."

"Then why?" He turned her to face him again, and his hand lingered against the silk-covered back of her neck.

She shrugged. "I guess we all want what we didn't have as a child."

"And a foster child only gets hand-me-downs."

Confusion rippled across her face. "No." She frowned. "That's not what I meant."

He ran his fingers over her robe, eventually allowing them to brush her soft neck. "Then why? I don't understand."

"It's not important." She took a step backward but he moved with her, unwilling or perhaps unable to break the contact.

Suddenly he wanted to know everything there was to know about Katherine Jackson. Not the dry statistics he'd learned from her background check, but who she really was. He inched his body closer to hers. "It's important to me."

She flattened herself against a bolt of red velour, her expression an alluring mix of fear and desire. "My first foster mother—" She shook her head. "I wanted to learn— The woman in the first family I was placed with was a seamstress."

He winced at the pain on Katherine's face. "She taught you?"

A second tear formed and slid down her cheek in the breath of a second. "No." She brushed the tear away, then looked down. "She wouldn't. I begged her, but she said there wasn't enough time. She said it wasn't worth it, that I wouldn't be there long enough."

He reached for her, stroking the side of her face until she returned his gaze.

"She was right," Katherine said. "I was there for less than six months."

"No. She wasn't right." Aaron reached out for the end of the red velour and brushed it against her face. Her eyes softened, and he thought she leaned slightly toward his touch.

But then she drew back, a sad smile playing about her lips. She gestured toward a top shelf filled with dusty how-to books and yellowed patterns. "My revenge."

He resisted the urge to reach for her, but his heart twisted with regret for all she'd endured, for how it should have been.

Katherine looked lost in thought as her gaze lingered on the books and patterns. "Maybe revenge isn't the right word." She shook her head. "It was more determination than anything else."

"You succeeded."

She smiled, nodding slowly. "I discarded a lot of ruined dresses and even more resentment along the way." When she met his gaze again, an old triumph sparkled. "What started out as something painful ended up as pleasure."

The only stitches Aaron was familiar with had come from football injuries, but he could imagine the sheer determination it would take to master such a difficult skill alone. And she had. He pictured a nine-year-old Katherine, alone and frightened. Anger rose up inside him. What would it have cost the woman to give her a little time, to lend some form of permanence to a child whose world no longer existed?

"Katherine . . ." Desire inched aside his protectiveness as he caught the sultry haze in her eyes. His touch went from comforting to seductive as his fingers tangled in her hair. He wanted to make things right for her. Hell, he wanted her. Period.

One hand fluttered protectively toward her chest, but she didn't push him away. He watched her fingers move in nervous motion against the base of her throat, and ached to press his lips there, see if she tasted as sweet as he imagined.

"Are you an orphan, a murderer, or a magician?" He fingered the lock of hair in order to contain his urge to touch her in places he had no right to touch. "You've certainly cast a spell over me. Who are you, Katherine Jackson?"

"I don't know," she whispered, her eyes shielded by an old pain. She moved his hand away. "I've been looking for the answer to that question all my life."

He glanced at her slender fingers wrapped around his wrist, and cursed himself as his desire for her flared nearly out of control. Damn the consequences. He pressed his body against hers until they were pushed into the soft folds of the red velour. It teased, shimmered behind him as he lowered his mouth to Katherine's ear.

"Then let me help you find out."

FIVE

Katherine gripped Aaron's shoulders as he whispered the words. A ripple of fear and anticipation ran through her as his scent—the clean smell of his T-shirt as his shoulder pressed closer, the irresistible scent of warm, male skin—literally made her head swim.

The entire situation was impossible, but she didn't push him away. She wanted him to kiss her, wanted it more than her next breath. Yet something within her rebelled at the idea of yielding so easily. His lips touched the side of her neck, lightly at first, then with more force. Her knees weakened at the hunger that rose within her. No, it wasn't a question of yielding; it was a question of when.

Her fingers curled against the thin material of his shirt as she felt the imprint of his holster against her breasts. The contact reminded her of who he was, what he thought she was capable of, and she forced herself to emerge from the sweet trance. Could she give even part of herself to someone who thought she was capable of murder?

She met his eyes as he drew back, waiting for her response. "And you want to help me find out who I am—"

Without warning, he lowered his head and brushed his lips across hers. The light abrasion of his unshaved jaw left her cheek tingling and her lips pulsing from the simple contact.

He pulled back. "Yes." The kiss had been brief—barely a kiss at all—yet the single word was spoken with determination, without hesitation.

Katherine felt her body respond, felt the seed of doubt begin to wither and die. He wasn't supposed to have responded that way. She had more to say, though she had to struggle to recall what it was. She forced her eyes open, needing to maintain some mental distance from the physical needs of her body. He watched her, obviously assessing her response to him.

Though she was certain her body was screaming something entirely different, she made herself speak the words she knew would break the spell. "Isn't it your job to find out who I am?" The expression on his face darkened, and she took a deep breath, willing herself to continue. "You're the professional, right?"

He grasped her hips and pulled them against his. His eyes never left hers, and she could see the white-hot fire behind them. "Does this feel professional to you?"

His arousal was evident, even through their clothes, and the slow, involuntary movement of her own hips made her body sink against his. She shook her head.

He lowered his mouth to her ear again and whispered. "Well, it doesn't feel professional to me either. That's the problem." He pulled away from her. "I've got to get out of here."

The spell was broken, leaving her cold. She wanted to suspend time, to recapture the intimacy they'd shared moments before. She'd never told a soul about the dresses, never imagined that she could share her reasons for making them.

"Wait." She heard the sharp edge to her own voice, the barely veiled panic. Suddenly she couldn't bear the thought of him leaving. At least not like this. "Don't go," she whispered.

He turned his back to her, his hands on his hips. "I've got to."

"Why?"

"Because if I stay—"

"If you stay, what?"

He faced her again. "You know as well as I do what will happen if I stay." He reached out and pressed the tips of his fingers against her cheek.

She raised her chin and said the only thing she could think of to stop him from leaving. "I dare you."

A glimmer of surprise lit his eyes. "Is that so? And why do you dare me, Katherine Jackson?"

She caught his hand. How could she make him understand? "Because I wanted that as much as you. Because . . ." Why had she cast his original suspicions back at him? "I think I tried to make you angry on purpose."

"I don't understand."

"I'm not used to having someone—" She broke the

sentence off, unable to find the right words. "Let's just say I've been alone for a long time, and then when someone finally drops into my life, he suspects me of murder. Is it just me, or is that ironic?"

"Do you really believe that I think you killed Owen Blake?"

She threw her hands into the air. "Of course I do, since you've said as much."

"No, that's not what I asked you. I asked you what you believed. Do you believe that I think you killed Owen Blake?"

Katherine looked into his ice-blue eyes, wishing she could see beyond the surface, wishing she could bridge the link they shared, touch the core of connection, and read his thoughts.

"Something tells me you haven't decided where I fit in yet."

He shrugged. "Maybe so. I'm a logical man. I operate on facts. I'm not comfortable with anything else."

She was willing to accept that explanation. At least for the moment. "If you leave here right now, where will you go?"

He grinned. "About forty yards away to my car outside."

"That's what I thought." She smiled. "Which means you're not as logical a man as you think you are, Detective Stone."

He grinned in earnest this time. "If I stay, do you promise we'll just sit around and drink tea and eat rice cakes, or whatever you people eat?"

"You people?" Her laughter was absorbed by the thick bolts of fabric stacked in the small space. "No, I can't promise you that." She placed her hand in the center of his chest and pushed him against a bolt of navy velvet. Standing on tiptoe, she leaned across him until her fingertips brushed against a sharp-edged box behind his right shoulder. "Got it," she said finally.

She felt the muscles of his chest tighten as she slid back into place. She presented him an almost-full box of Snickers candy bars.

"Is there a reason why you hide chocolate bars in your sewing room?" he asked, an amused expression on his face.

She shook her head. "The textbooks say that it's common for adults who had transient childhoods to hoard food." She took two candy bars out of the box before sliding it back onto the shelf and smiling at him. "I say it's just a darn good idea."

He didn't return her smile. "It must have been difficult for you."

Katherine recognized the seriousness of his expression, but only shrugged as she motioned for him to follow her from the sewing room. "Yes, it was. But I got through. It was never as hard as the first time. Whenever it was time to be placed with another family, I tried to envision myself as a Gypsy princess who was only off on another grand adventure."

He turned her by the shoulder as they reached the empty bedroom, pushing back a wayward tendril of hair before cupping her face between his large hands. "You are a Gypsy princess," he said softly.

Katherine wanted to say something, wanted to tell him that no one had ever said anything so beautiful to her, had never made her feel the way he did. But she didn't have the words. Instead she welcomed his body against hers as he pinned her to the bedroom wall.

His kiss wasn't gentle this time, it was hungry. Hungry for her, she thought as he parted her lips, his tongue meeting hers with impatient thrusts. He tasted like she'd imagined—and touched her like a fantasy, warm and slick, expertly commanding. And hard, she thought as his hips pressed against hers.

The thought of his body craving hers as she longed for his made each breath difficult. She felt her nipples tighten, and a ragged moan from deep in Aaron's throat told her he'd felt her body respond.

Her shoulder bumped the light switch, then the bedroom went dark. Aaron pulled back, hesitating.

"It's all right." She twisted to find the switch, but he stopped her by pulling her face back toward his.

"Don't," he whispered as his hands slid up her sides, searching. Nothing but a fresh swell of desire penetrated the darkness as he found her breasts. He ran his hands along the outside of her silky robe, pausing to caress her hardened nipples.

With the darkness came a certain freedom to explore, and Katherine traced the outline of Aaron's body, feeling her way up his shoulders, resting her hands against the base of his neck. He hesitated, as if sensing her need to touch him. She made a strangled sound as she combed her fingers into his hair. Without realizing it, she'd longed to feel the silky texture of his dark hair, coil the loose waves between her fingers.

Her chance to explore ended abruptly as Aaron parted her robe and slipped his hands inside. Flesh burned against flesh as his fingers branded their imprint on her exposed breasts.

The sound of persistent barking permeated the room despite the closed windows and eventually roused Katherine from the heady drug that was Aaron Stone. They broke away from each other, both obviously interrupted by the same thing.

Aaron's hands moved to her shoulders as he looked toward the window, his breathing still rapid. "That's not Roscoe, is it?" he asked.

She readjusted her robe and walked to the window. He trailed her, one hand possessively circling her upper arm. "No," she answered. "He's asleep somewhere inside. Probably in my bed, if I know him."

Aaron joined her in peering through the miniblinds to the street below. The streetlamp cast its dull bluish light across her lawn, then slanted, though faintly, across the street as well.

"What the hell—" Aaron had obviously spotted the same dark figure she had. He was in motion as the figure ducked behind his sedan.

"Wait." Her voice halted him midway across the room. "It's probably just our neighbor." She motioned for him to join her again at the window. "He works the night shift."

Aaron seemed worried. "Are you sure?"

She could sense the tension in his body as he stood beside her.

"He has a whole passel of kids," she continued. "And they must own a hundred bicycles and tricycles between them."

She touched his arm lightly, longing to recapture

the passion they'd shared just moments before, but knowing it was better this way, better that they'd stopped. At least that's what the logical side of her brain argued.

"He's probably just picking up one of the toys."

Aaron grunted and continued to watch the street below. Suddenly he let the blind snap back into place. "Ah hell!"

"What is it?" She parted the blind and peered down toward the street, but nothing looked out of place.

Aaron was rubbing his forehead as if the gesture could fix whatever was wrong. He finally looked up. "Can I use your phone?" He smiled at her surprised expression. "You just reminded me that I forgot to call my brother."

"You forgot to call your brother," she repeated. Grabbing his wrist, she tilted the face of his watch toward her. "It's four o'clock in the morning."

"Good," Aaron said as if something had just occurred to him. "He'll be awake."

A million questions flooded her mind. So Aaron had a brother. What was his name? Why was he awake at four in the morning? A nagging feeling in the pit of her stomach reminded Katherine that she didn't really know Aaron at all, but she pushed it aside, not willing to destroy the magic of the last few minutes.

She pointed toward the doorway. "There's a phone in my bedroom and one in the kitchen."

Katherine returned to the window as Aaron left the room. She thought she spotted the figure move behind an overgrown forsythia shrub on the street corner, but after watching the spot intently for a few moments, she decided she must have been mistaken. She smiled as the sound of Aaron's voice reached her. His laughter was clear, though she couldn't make out what he was saying. She was drawn toward the sound, and she guiltily answered the craving to know more about him, as she edged toward the hallway.

". . . I know, I know," she heard him say. "You'll have to explain to Mother about the case." He sighed. "There's just no way in hell I can leave town right now." He paused, obviously listening. "Don't you think I'd rather eat watermelon and shoot fireworks with the brats than pull surveillance?"

Watermelon . . . the Fourth of July . . . surveillance . . . Irrational anger surged inside her. She balled her fists once, then twice, before it subsided. Was he afraid she'd skip town, or could it simply be that he didn't want to leave her? It was impossible to tell from the tone of his voice.

"I've just got too much pending. . . . Tell everyone I'll make it next time." The click of the receiver being placed back into its cradle sounded down the hall.

Katherine approached her bedroom with silent determination. She found Aaron sitting on the edge of the bed, rubbing Roscoe's ears as intensely as he'd rubbed his own forehead. He jumped as she stopped in the doorway, frustration etched in every handsome detail of his face.

"Am I what you have pending?" she asked. She knew the answer was yes, but some perverse, curious part of her had to know exactly why Aaron still thought he should keep her under surveillance.

The smile he flashed in her direction didn't hint at an answer. Instead it caused a familiar heat to flow across her. "Hey, don't we have a date with late-night television and a Snickers bar?"

She shook her head, ready to dig her anger out from underneath the generous helping of charm he'd just applied.

He crossed the room and looped his arm around her shoulders. "So what's on television at this time of night—I mean day?"

"Static and televangelists," she replied evenly. "You're canceling plans with your family to keep an eye on me, aren't you? You're afraid I'll skip town."

"It's not like that, exactly."

She turned toward him, refusing to budge when he tried to urge her forward. "Are you still that suspicious of me?"

"Katherine—" The high-pitched sound of his beeper saved him from a response, not that he had one. Aaron lifted the pager from his belt, and his pulse quickened as he recognized the telephone number lit up on the digital face. "Can I—?"

Katherine hooked her thumb toward her bedroom. "Be my guest."

He suppressed the urge to kiss her one last time before he answered the page. How had things gotten so intimate between them so quickly? Hell, he couldn't remember the last time he'd felt this at ease, this familiar with a woman. He clenched his jaw, angry at himself for the emotions that were coursing through him.

Emotions he'd foolishly allowed himself to feel for Katherine. Well, the call he was about to make could easily change everything.

It might even prove that the woman he ached to make love to was a murderer.

"I'll be right back," he muttered as he headed toward the phone.

Suddenly the last thing he wanted to do was to pick up the receiver and dial the number to forensics. He did it anyway.

"Anderson," a man answered in a familiar squeaky voice.

If Aaron hadn't known the voice belonged to a burly, six-foot-two man, he would have sworn it belonged to a sixteen-year-old girl. Michael Anderson's voice would have earned him the nickname Mickey, even if his first name hadn't helped matters along.

"Mickey. Aaron Stone here. You got something for me?"

"Hey—did I wake you? You said you wanted me to page you as soon as we had anything."

Aaron shook his head, annoyed at Mickey's apology, at delaying the inevitable. "No, you didn't wake me. What did you find?"

"One, the fingerprints I lifted from the duct tape weren't found on Owen Blake's body. Two, it looks like we're going to have to place the time of death a little earlier than what we'd first thought. That idiot rookie turned the air conditioner off at the scene, and no one bothered to tell me it had been on until—"

"So what's the time of death now?"

"I'm estimating between noon and six o'clock Saturday afternoon."

So, the time of death could be confirmed as late Saturday afternoon. He suppressed the dangerous urge to totally dismiss his suspicion of Katherine. Her whereabouts had been confirmed as working the counter at the herb shop at that time, but that still didn't answer all his questions.

Like why she'd called the inn in the first place.

Aaron rubbed his forehead to clear his thoughts. No, he might not have acted professionally in the last couple of days, but he couldn't afford to throw caution to the wind now. "Were you able to lift any additional prints from the tape?"

"Sorry. No additional ones other than yours."

That meant no evidence of a perp—no hard evidence that Katherine hadn't staged the break-in in an attempt to deflect suspicion. Still, something in him rallied at the news from forensics. Facts were facts, and in this case they were backing up his instincts. But forensics could be a few hours off in its estimation of the time of death. And with the evidence hinging on something as fragile as an air-conditioning unit . . .

His mind drifted to the first time he'd seen Katherine. She'd been sitting in the convertible with Roscoe, the top down, in full view, munching a hamburger. He would have laughed at the image, but it was replaced by the memory of the break-in. She'd been visibly shaken that night, terrified, in fact. And when he'd held her, their bodies had fit so perfectly. . . .

He shook his head. Katherine couldn't have murdered Owen Blake. But she still might know who did. . . .

"Aaron?" Mickey's voice interrupted his thoughts.

"Yeah, I'm here. Sorry. Listen, I owe you one, Mickey."

"Sure thing. But next time tell that rookie not to screw with the air conditioner or anything else."

"I'll do that." Aaron was already laying the phone down as Mickey launched himself into a predictable squeaky frenzy about compromising the crime scene.

Aaron rose from the bed and made his way to the living room, where Katherine was fumbling through a stack of videos piled next to a small television. Her straight dark hair literally spewed from the ponytail holder atop her head, then cascaded almost to the floor as she bent over. On any other woman it would have looked comical, but on Katherine it looked appealing, if not downright seductive.

Unnoticed, he allowed himself to observe her for a moment. The background check he'd run told him she'd lived at this address for fifteen years. Her record was spotless. He looked around the apartment at the jungle of plants, at the amethyst-colored geode that sat atop her electric bill on the coffee table, the sheepskin rug lying next to the sofa for her dog. A murderer? Not if he had one instinct left in his body.

Okay, he reasoned, so what if Katherine was involved somehow in Owen Blake's murder? If, as he'd once suspected, she had contacts within the department, she'd know everything there was to know about him. That included his family. If that was the case, he'd be better off keeping an eye on her. What was it they said—keep your friends close, your enemies even closer?

"How do you feel about fireworks?" he asked.

She looked up, a confused expression on her face. "Right now, or in general?"

"Right now."

She scratched her head. "It's after four in the morning."

"Okay, okay." He had to shove his hands into his pockets to keep from reaching for her. "How would you feel about fireworks after, say, a few hours' sleep?"

"Uh—okay, I guess." She tossed a video onto the sofa and stood to face him.

"Good. That way I won't have to beg forgiveness from my family for the next year."

"Wait. Are you asking me to your family's Fourth of July get-together?"

"Yes."

She blinked at him. "Okay," she finally answered.

Aaron couldn't think of another response, so he nodded. "Good. Set your alarm and get some sleep." He moved toward the door. "I'll be back to pick you up at ten. Oh—and bring your swimsuit."

She smiled faintly. "Anything else?"

"Not unless you feel inclined to pack a candy bar or two."

His crystal-blue gaze held promise and love. A love never spoken of, but there all the same. "Stay with me, please."

Of course it was Aaron. The thought of not recognizing

him now seemed ludicrous. Aaron—her savior. Pure of heart, the purest of intentions. But he didn't understand.

She felt the fine hairs on the back of her neck rise. Danger. She shook her head. No, she could never let him hurt Aaron. Aaron would defend her until the end—or until one of them was dead. Of that she was certain.

Bile rose in her throat at the thought of Aaron losing his life. He was so young, so full of the goodness that had somehow passed her by.

"Why won't you stay with me tonight?" he asked again, his fingertips stroking her bruised cheekbone. "You can't stay here."

She flinched, but not from the pain. Even after the last few months, she couldn't get used to the tenderness of his touch. He wanted more, would give her more than friendship if she'd let him. He could love her, she thought, and felt the tears she'd held in check spill over her swollen cheek, sting the split that marred her lower lip.

She shook her head. No—he'd find them, kill them. Hadn't he always managed to find her when she ran? She would never put Aaron in that kind of danger.

"I can't," she said, her voice quivering like a child's. Or an old woman's, she thought. Yes, more like an old woman's.

For a moment he allowed the rage to show, then masked it. For her benefit, of course, she thought. Then he pulled her trembling hands into his and laid his head against their entwined fingers.

"Please let me take care of you," he whispered. "Please, Jacqueline."

Katherine woke with a start, practically leaping off the bed as she sat upright. She touched her face, not at all surprised that her cheeks were damp with tears. The dream had been so real that she'd almost expected to find her face bruised, her lower lip cut and swollen. Her hands were trembling, and she clasped them together. What on earth was going on?

She had a feeling it was not only something very real, it was very important. To her, to Aaron . . . and to a woman named Jacqueline.

"*If I find you snooping around in my past again* . . ." Aaron's words echoed through her head.

He had been with her in the dream, but Katherine had obviously not been the woman. She'd merely been privy to the other woman's thoughts, her emotions. The woman's name had definitely been Jacqueline.

And Aaron was in love with her.

At that moment she realized what a gift Aaron's love would be. Luckily, Roscoe rescued her from considering the thought further as he squeezed his long body between her feet.

"Good morning to you too," she said in a distracted voice. She rewarded Roscoe with a thorough ear scratching before making her way into the kitchen and opening the door to let him outside. Her muscles felt stiff, cramped as she walked, and she realized that her body had probably been as tense as a clothesline while she slept. Leave it to an insomniac to find a way around restful sleep, she thought as she stuffed a coffee filter into the coffeemaker and shoveled in three heaping tablespoons of coffee.

Two cups of coffee and a long, hot shower later, she

was feeling as good as she was going to after two hours of sleep. Perversely her alarm clock sounded as she started to carry her now-empty coffee cup to the kitchen.

"Why do I own you?" she snapped as she hit the off button and sat down on the bed.

She was rarely at ease with people she didn't know, and normally an invitation like Aaron's would have her stomach in knots. But this morning all she could think about was the dream. Absently she touched her cheek. She could count on one hand the number of bad bumps and bruises she'd encountered in her life, and none of them had been at the hand of someone else.

Was the dream just a fabrication, some fictional extension of the first dream? It seemed as real to her as anything she'd ever experienced. She closed her eyes, allowing her mind to relive it. Fear enveloped her, sending goose bumps scattering across her bare arms and legs. She felt vulnerable, and longed to put on something more than the denim shorts and cropped summer top that she wore.

She eased her legs onto the mattress instead. Dread. That was what she was feeling. She dreaded the future, couldn't bear to think about the past. This was all she—Jacqueline—had known for so long that she couldn't imagine it any other way.

Jacqueline? Katherine's own awareness surfaced for a moment, but she allowed her mind to drift back to Jacqueline, welcomed the other woman's thoughts as her own.

Happiness? Yes, she had been happy as a child. But that had been so long ago. Her cheekbone throbbed, and her lip felt grotesquely swollen against the touch of her tongue.

And Aaron . . . He had been there watching her, expecting her to do the right thing, to leave with him. She loved him for that, but he had no idea what that choice—her choice—could do to him. The last thread of bravery swelled within her. It was still her choice to leave—or stay—with the monster who was her husband.

A small cry escaped her. She might not be able to save herself, but she would save Aaron.

As if from a long distance away she heard pounding.

"Katherine?" a voice—Aaron's voice—called. Closer now. "Katherine?"

She jumped as a warm hand clasped her upper arm. "It's just me." Her eyes flew open, and she saw Aaron standing over her, a look of concern wrinkling his brow. "Are you okay?"

Katherine swallowed down the surge of fear that had been so close just moments before, and resisted the urge to throw her arms around Aaron. She sat up, cradling her forehead in her hands. "Yeah, I'm okay. I guess I just drifted back off," she lied.

The fact that she hadn't drifted back to sleep sent a shiver down her spine. It was the first time she had felt the connection to Aaron while she was awake. *Who is Jacqueline?* she wanted to shout. *Do you still love her?*

"I'm early." He sat down beside her and pulled her hands from her face. "Didn't you hear me knocking?"

She feigned a smile and shrugged. "No, I'm sorry, I didn't. How did you get in?"

He inclined his head toward the kitchen. "Roscoe

let me in." His expression grew serious. "Lock it next time."

"Right." She tried to hide the roller-coaster emotions that were running through her as she rose from the bed. "Let me throw a few things in a day bag and I'll be ready. Should we bring something?"

"Buns," he replied without hesitation. "That's all they ever make the bachelor bring."

Her breath caught in her throat as she watched Aaron stretch out on her bed. Was this the man who had accused her of murder just days ago? He'd changed into a pair of denim shorts and a T-shirt, and his long legs were masculine perfection with their distracting blend of muscle and dark hair.

She struggled to find something to say as he pulled her pillow onto his chest as if it were the most natural thing in the world. "I-I take it you don't cook?" she stammered.

He grazed his jaw against the soft cotton of her pillowcase, and she thought she saw a flash of desire in his eyes. But as soon as it was there it was gone, replaced by an amused grin. "Of course I do. I just don't want them to know." He met her puzzled look. "They'll stop letting me just bring buns."

An hour later Aaron pulled his teal-blue pickup truck, which Katherine decided better suited him than the sedan, onto a seemingly endless gravel drive. They'd made the trip to his brother's lake house in relative silence, but it felt natural to enjoy being with Aaron without the need for words.

In reality, they barely knew each other. But then again, theirs wasn't your average relationship. When someone suspected you of murder, ran background checks, and put you under constant surveillance, it tended to accelerate the intimacy level.

Katherine stole a glance at Aaron's profile. Something had changed. She couldn't pinpoint exactly what, but she would bet her life savings it had to do with the telephone call he'd made early that morning. If only she could summon whatever strange connection she shared with Aaron on command. She steadied herself against the seat as the pickup made a sharp turn. Too bad it didn't seem to work that way.

"So are you ready to meet the Stone clan?"

She glanced up to see a neat two-story brick house nestled in a wide expanse of freshly mowed lawn. The lawn was surrounded by a natural frame of ancient oak trees, their massive limbs casting tempting shade across the grass. A crisp, clean American flag flew from the upper story porch, making the scene look like a well-planned postcard.

The flutter of butterflies began, then settled in her stomach as she clasped her hands in her lap. "Clan? You make it sound like there's a whole village of you."

He grinned in her direction. "No, not nearly that many. I only have five brothers and sisters."

"Five brothers and sisters!" she repeated. "Your parents have six kids?" Sheer terror rose from the pit of her stomach. What was she going to do—to say—to five of Aaron's siblings? Not to mention his parents. Then a terrible thought hit her. "Have you told them about me, about the case?" A quick glance at him told her the answer was yes.

"Only David," he replied evenly. "My oldest brother." He nodded toward the house. "This is his place."

Katherine cradled her head in her hands. She had been quietly dreading socializing with Aaron's family. After all, what did she know about family? Mike had practically had one foot out the door to join the air force when she'd arrived at Walt and Grams's, and heaven knows, he'd made a point of avoiding her ever since. She swallowed down the disappointment she felt whenever she thought of Mike, of his two beautiful girls and new baby—children she longed to call her family, but couldn't. A sad smile crossed her lips. Children she had never even seen.

And now at least one of Aaron's siblings knew she was involved in a murder case. She glanced at Aaron again. The expression on his face was relaxed, and his eyes no longer crinkled with suspicion when he looked at her. Was it possible she wasn't a suspect anymore? It was probably wishful thinking, but she couldn't shake the thought. Still, her secret didn't exactly put her best foot forward with David.

Aaron parked the truck next to a line of other vehicles. They ranged from a boxy older model Oldsmobile to an unabashedly expensive Mercedes. And, she noted with amusement, there was a shiny black motorcycle with a pink tricycle parked next to it, mimicking its position right down to the exact angle of the handlebars.

When Aaron hopped out of the pickup and circled

around it to open her door, Katherine found she didn't even have the nerve to unbuckle her seat belt.

He frowned. "You look like you'd rather be anywhere else than here."

You're right—let's go, she thought. But for once she didn't say the first thing that popped into her head. She met his questioning gaze. "It's just that I'm not very comfortable . . . I don't know much about families this size."

To her surprise Aaron leaned over and kissed her soundly, his big hand cupping her face and his tongue exploring her lips, then moving inside her mouth with barely checked hunger. He finally pulled away with a low moan. "The good thing about a family this size is that no one notices if you slip away for a while."

Katherine couldn't help but smile, yet she wondered which was worse: butterflies or the unsatisfied hunger that Aaron's kiss had left coursing through her. She unlatched her seat belt and hopped from the truck. "Okay. Let's go," she said with more confidence than she felt.

Aaron scooped up his grocery sack filled with hamburger buns, then looped his arm around her shoulders. "For the purpose of everyone here, except David, you're my date. Nothing more."

She felt a stab of uncertainty. Had he only invited her to keep an eye on her? No. She touched her fingertips to her lips. She wasn't certain of everything where Detective Aaron Stone was concerned, but she knew he wanted more from her than answers.

SIX

The peaceful scene that greeted them turned out to be a facade of sorts, as she and Aaron walked around the house to the lakefront. A group of young children, all clad in brightly colored bathing suits, were squealing and running in different directions on the lawn. Katherine smiled as she spotted the source of their laughter: a lawn sprinkler. Before her was the most magnificent view of any lake she'd ever seen, seemingly endless water that sparkled with the noonday sun, yet the children's focus was on a small stream of oscillating water.

Aaron reached out and snagged a dark-haired girl of about five, and held her squirming, thoroughly wet body out in front of him. "Katy. Give your favorite uncle a kiss and then say hi to my friend Katherine."

The little girl pursed her lips for a quick kiss from Aaron. "Hi," she said, smiling in Katherine's direction before kicking her legs in an effort to get down and rejoin the others.

Katherine smiled at the group of children as Katy

ran and jumped across the spray of water. "She's beautiful."

"She is that." Aaron shook his head. "But mean as a snake, that one. David expects her to march on Washington any day now."

"No, she couldn't be mean. She has the face of an angel."

"So does my sister Desiree." Aaron pushed up his shirtsleeve and pointed to a jagged white scar on his upper arm. "But see that? When we were kids—"

"Honestly, Aaron," a silky smooth voice interrupted. "Are you ever going to get over that?"

Katherine looked up to find a woman who, indeed, had the face of an angel. Large blue eyes dominated a heart-shaped face, and soft ringlets of long chestnut hair fell across her slender shoulders. She was a feminine version of Aaron, Katherine realized, and had to be Desiree.

"Sneaking up on me." Aaron held the scar up for closer inspection. "That's how she did this in the first place. We were on vacation, and I was sitting on the pier fishing—minding my own business—when she pushed me in."

"And there was a rusty nail sticking out that gave him a horrible, life-threatening cut. We were all amazed that he didn't die." Desiree reached around Katherine and tugged Aaron's shirtsleeve back into place before giving him a solid push. "Get over it, will you?"

Aaron stumbled on the uneven ground before finding solid footing. He barely contained a smile as he pointed at Desiree. "See? I told you she was mean."

Desiree ignored her brother and extended her hand to Katherine. "In case you haven't figured it out, I'm Desiree."

Katherine reached out to take the other woman's hand. She was as tall as Katherine, but slender to the point of seeming fragile. "I thought so," she replied, unsure what to think of the banter between brother and sister. "I'm Katherine."

Desiree's face lit up with a genuine smile. "It's nice to meet you." She pointed to the group of giggling children. "The little blond linebacker is mine," she said with pride. "His name is Jonathan."

Katherine glanced at the chubby blond boy of about two, then back at the wispy thin, dark-haired Desiree. "Are you sure?" she asked with a smile.

Desiree gestured toward a gazebo at the edge of the lawn, where a handsome, muscular young man was turning a water spigot, obviously adjusting the water pressure for the children. His sandy blond hair glistened in the sun as he gave a small wave. "That's Greg." Desiree smiled. "He's mine too."

"Now I see." Katherine laughed, thinking both Desiree and her husband Greg seemed familiar. "Could we have met before?"

"Mm . . . probably not in person." Desiree shook her head. "But I've done some modeling, and Greg played football for Florida State a few years back."

Aaron handed Desiree his grocery sack. "Here. Make yourself useful and take this to the kitchen." He draped his arm around Katherine's shoulders. "I want to introduce Katherine."

"Sure." Desiree peeked into the sack. "Let me

guess . . ." she mumbled as she walked up the incline toward the house. "Buns?"

Katherine looked up at the house and stopped dead in her tracks. "Are all of those people your family?"

Aaron looked, too, seeming for the first time to take notice of the crowd of people watching them. "Uh-huh," he replied casually. "But it doesn't look like everyone's arrived yet."

Not everyone? she thought, forcing one foot in front of the other as Aaron urged her forward.

An older couple emerged from the crowd as she and Aaron topped the incline to a covered patio. The woman was petite, with short-cropped silver hair, warm brown eyes, and an even smile. She hugged Aaron soundly. "Hi, hon. We're so glad you were able to come." Then she grasped Katherine's hands. "You must be Katherine."

Aaron interrupted before Katherine could respond. "Katherine, this is Mom and Pop Stone."

Aaron's mother wagged a finger in his direction. "I've told you not to call us that. For heaven's sake! It makes us sound like some defunct rock band."

Katherine couldn't help but laugh, and knew in that instant that she was going to like Aaron's mother. "It's nice to meet you, Mrs. Stone."

Aaron's father stepped forward, and Katherine was struck by his resemblance to Aaron and Desiree. He had Aaron's tall, solid frame, the same luminescent eyes and dark lashes, but with a thick crop of silver hair. It was obvious whose genes had surfaced in the family tree.

"Katherine, we're glad you could join us," he said

with an incline of his head. He glanced over his shoulder at a man tending a barbecue grill. "David is tied up at the moment . . ."

Katherine glanced nervously toward the grill to find a dark-headed, broad-shouldered man waving in her direction.

". . . so I'll say it for him—make yourself right at home," Aaron's father finished.

"Thank you." Katherine waved at David, then clasped her hands together. "David's home is beautiful."

And indeed it was. As a child she'd dreamed of living in a place like this. Overhead fans created a silent breeze on the covered patio, and from inside the stately brick house came the tantalizing smell of potato salad and baked beans. It wasn't just a house, she realized. It was a home.

Yes, she'd dreamed of living in a house like this, but she'd also dreamed of having a *family* like this. She hadn't, though. And now she didn't fit in, didn't quite know what to say to these people who oddly seemed so interested in her. She willed herself to calm down, to relax.

"Marie," Aaron called as he peered around his parents. "I know you're dying to get up here, so come on." He squeezed Katherine's shoulder and laughed softly. "If there's enough room."

She saw instantly what he meant as a very pretty, very pregnant Marie made her way through the crowd. At her elbow was, Katherine presumed, her husband. He guided her past the tangle of family members, and didn't remove his hand from her arm even when they stopped.

"Katherine, this is my sister Marie." Aaron cleared his throat. "And her husband, Calvin."

Calvin and Marie simultaneously held out their hands for a handshake, then both burst out laughing at the same time.

Aaron shook his head and whispered into Katherine's ear, "I would say that they're joined at the hip, but it's painfully obvious that they've been joined elsewhere as well."

Katherine was certain her face went three shades of red. She grasped Marie's outstretched hand, then Calvin's. "It's nice to meet the two . . . uh, the three of you." She nodded toward the other woman's rounded belly. "When are you due?"

"She's overdue." A worried frown split Calvin's forehead. "The doctor says she's two centimeters and twenty percent effaced," he said in a breathless voice.

Beside her, Aaron made a small choking sound. "Calvin, I thought it looked like Megan was getting a little too much sun," he said as he craned his neck in the direction of the playing children.

The worried crease on Calvin's face deepened. "Oh no! Honey, where did you put the sunscreen?"

"Oh, I knew it!" Marie said as she began looking around. "She's so fair. Like you, Calvin." She turned to Katherine and Aaron. "I'm so sorry to run off, but we need to put another application of sunscreen on Meggie."

"No problem," Aaron assured them in a serious tone.

Katherine turned to him as his sister and brother-in-law scrambled off, side by side, sunscreen in hand. "You are awful," she whispered.

"What? What did I do?"

She gave him an accusing sideways glance.

"In case you didn't realize it, you were about to get a thirty-minute obstetric dissertation." He answered her question before she could ask it. "No, he's not an obstetrician. He's a plumber."

Katherine stifled a laugh and pretended to adjust her earring.

Aaron let go of her shoulder long enough to pluck a potato chip from a glass bowl that was centered on a beige rattan table. "Faith—"

Katherine turned to find a woman, newborn baby on her shoulder, rocking in an old-fashioned wooden porch rocker. She held one finger up to her lips to silence Aaron.

"Sorry," Aaron mouthed. He pointed to the woman and child. "This is Faith, my oldest sister," he told Katherine in a quiet voice. "And the little one is Rae."

Faith adjusted the baby's ruffled pink sleeper and pointed wordlessly at the group of children.

Aaron nodded. "Oh yeah. Two of those little heathens—Nathan and Maddie—are hers." He turned back to his sister. "Where's your better half?" he asked, his voice low.

"Robert's somewhere with Raece," she whispered.

Aaron lowered his mouth to Katherine's ear. "Raece is my youngest brother, David is the oldest—"

"Coming through," a thunderous deep voice declared, drawing an incredulous eye roll from Faith.

"Honestly, David!" she whispered.

David placed a platter of freshly grilled hamburgers and hot dogs on the table. "My apologies, Madam Faith," he said, bowing deeply, a blue floral oven mitt on one hand.

Faith kicked at him, but missed, too busy balancing the sleeping baby to do any real harm. Katherine felt her discomfort fading. They were all so at ease with one another. Her gaze danced over Aaron's parents, who were busy arranging paper plates and plastic dinnerware, then skimmed the dark-headed adults who were Aaron's brothers and sisters. How many times had she looked in the mirror, wondering what a brother or sister of her own would look like? Wondering, if her mother weren't dead, what resemblance she might find in her face.

Aaron held out a cushioned rattan chair for her. "Have a seat, and I'll fix us something to eat." She started to protest, but he silenced her with a wave and pointed toward the French doors. "Can you see in there?"

Inside was a wild jumble of kids, food-laden paper plates, and dripping bathing suits. Katherine laughed. "I see what you mean. I take my burgers all the way."

He was back in an instant, balancing two paper plates mounded with hamburgers, potato salad, and baked beans. Mrs. Stone was right behind him with two glasses of lemonade.

Aaron looked up at his mother. "I keep trying to

convince her not to call the little heathens to lunch until we're through, but she won't have it."

Mrs. Stone smacked Aaron soundly on the back of the head. "Honestly, Aaron. Would you please not call my precious grandchildren names?"

At that moment the kids, as if by collective agreement, ran from the house, through and around the legs of the adults, and jumped back into the sprinklers. Mrs. Stone smiled. "God love 'em, the little heathens," she muttered as she headed back toward the kitchen.

Katherine watched as David followed little Katy with a dry towel. He seemed like a big kid himself, totally lovable, huggable, and not at all the type she imagined would live in such an expensive-looking house. There was a down-to-earth, responsible quality about him that touched her.

She turned toward Aaron. "How long has David's wife been dead?" she asked.

Aaron's eyes darkened to a dangerous shade of navy, and Katherine knew instantly what she'd done, what she'd said . . . what she'd known.

"I don't recall mentioning that," he said flatly, his voice low.

She swallowed the bite of hamburger that had turned to a rock in her mouth. In that split second she considered all sorts of options, including lying to him. In the end, she opted for the truth.

"I don't think you did mention it." Setting her fork down, she looked Aaron in the eye. She lowered her voice so that, hopefully, only Aaron would be aware of the awkward drama that was playing out between them. "Maybe it was that he was caring for the children by himself, or maybe it was one of those things I just seem to know. I honestly don't know the difference between my perceptiveness and my abilities sometimes."

Aaron glanced at his brother and the children. David had directed Martin and Alexander to put their swim shoes back on, and was busy drying off Katy's hair and pulling it into a ponytail. He nodded and took another bite of hamburger, seemingly satisfied with her answer.

Katherine breathed a sigh of relief. She didn't want to analyze her feelings for Aaron—didn't want to admit that whether or not he believed her had become the most important thing on earth to her. And that, to her surprise, spending this day with Aaron and his family filled a deep void in her.

She didn't want to admit it because that void would be back tomorrow.

"Susan died from a brain hemorrhage three years ago." Aaron's voice snapped her back to the present. "There was no way to know it was going to happen." His voice reflected the pain of loss, though she was certain he attempted to mask it with the carefully chosen words.

She watched David with his three children. "I'm sorry," she said, and the words seemed inadequate even to her.

"David's tough." Aaron shook his head. "He moved his office into the house so that he could be with the children. He works crazy hours, never sleeps. But he's making it."

"Snake! Snake!" The children began to squeal. "Nathan has a snake!"

"Oh Lord," Faith muttered as she rose to her feet.

Aaron was out of his chair in a flash, running across the lawn toward the screaming children.

Katherine automatically held out her arms for the baby, and Faith, just as naturally, placed the sleeping Rae on Katherine's shoulder before taking off in the direction of the children.

Katherine was thankful she'd loosely French-braided her long hair, as the baby nestled her soft cheek against the curve of her neck. For one panicky moment, she didn't know what to do, how to hold the precious bundle that was so trusting—and so tiny. She gently laid her hand between Rae's shoulder blades, comforted by the easy rise and fall of the baby's breathing. She was so incredibly small, she realized, and yet so powerful.

Powerful because Rae was the cause of the overwhelming maternal longing that was surging through her body. How long had it been since she'd held an infant? Probably as long as it had been since she'd admitted that her heart—her body—longed for a child of her own. Katherine sighed as the sweet baby smell of lotion and clean skin reached her nose. Her fingertips circled against the supple cotton of the infant sleeper, then found the soft roll of skin at the nape of the baby's neck.

She watched Faith smile broadly as she reached the circle of children. Aaron looked in her direction and held up a squirming green garden snake. Katherine watched the scene through a veil of sweet emotion. She waved in their direction, then closed her eyes, rocking back and forth as Rae made a cooing noise. Everything else faded—the children's voices, the snake, the accusation she'd seen earlier in Aaron's eyes.

"Thanks so much, Katherine." The voice was Faith's.

The baby was Faith's.

Katherine's eyes flew open, the moment lost to her forever. She watched as Faith automatically slung a cloth diaper over her left shoulder, then reached for Rae. Katherine barely had time to react before Faith lifted the baby from her shoulder and easily settled her back in the proper place—on her mother's shoulder.

Katherine blinked back emotion. Now certainly wasn't the time, and this wasn't the place, to face deeply buried longings. If there was ever a right place and time. She didn't know anymore. Was it worth it to examine unfulfilled yearnings, when there was no answer to the pain in sight?

She allowed herself one long, hard look at her life. She wasn't unhappy, but neither was she happy. She was content. Working at the Herb Shop made her content. She was good at it, enjoyed it, worked hard. The ties she felt to customers and friends, to Walt and Grams, filled a need inside her.

At least partially.

Katherine felt an old panic rise inside her. For most of her life she'd avoided looking too closely at her own needs. Dreams? She hadn't allowed herself any. Sewing made her happy, but even that pleasure had been born of pain. Still, the act of creating—of turning plain bolts of fabric and thread into something beautiful—made her happy. At least while she was lost in the task. Invariably, though, the project would be completed and the emptiness would return.

"Nathan refuses to let it go," Faith said softly beside her. "Aaron has gone to find a mason jar to put it in. Now, what, exactly, I'm going to do with the snake when I get home, I have no idea. Ah—now they show up." Faith nodded toward two men who were strolling in the children's direction. "My husband, Robert, and my wayward brother Raece."

It took a moment for Katherine to realize that Faith was talking to her. Then she followed Faith's gaze to Aaron, Robert, and Raece. The men took turns holding the harmless snake, periodically extending it close to the children and eliciting squeals of pretend terror from the group. She felt a growing discomfort form within her, and shuddered with self-condemnation as she recognized it for what it was: jealousy.

It would be all too easy to feel a part of this family, of this day. And all too soon it would be ripped away from her. Surveillance, she reminded herself. No matter what cloak of disguise he used, and regardless of whether his attraction went any deeper than mere lust, that was what this was. What she was. Part and parcel of the job.

She heard a soft rustle of fabric, and looked up to find Mrs. Stone handing a glass of lemonade to Faith. Aaron's mother paused to caress baby Rae's peach-fuzz hair before settling into a rattan chair next to Katherine.

"I see Robert and Raece have made it back."

Katherine looked at the two men. She didn't have to ask which was Robert and which was Aaron's brother Raece. Raece, though his hair was cut radically short, had inherited the same dark hair as the other five Stone siblings. His features resembled David's though his build was far slimmer than either brother's.

Faith laughed softly. "Once again they must have given away all the fish they caught."

Aaron's mother cast a loving glance at her family, then turned to Katherine. "Raece and Robert take their fishing very seriously." Her brown eyes warmed as she smoothed a lock of hair from her forehead. "They accuse the children of distracting them, so if they manage to sneak off by themselves they have to blame something else."

"What do you think it will be today?" Faith asked.

Mrs. Stone glanced upward. "The sun's too bright," she said with a smile.

Something within Katherine twisted with longing, and it took all her energy not to bolt from the chair. Just being with Aaron's mother, seeing her calm acceptance of her children, made an unexpected sadness settle about her shoulders and weigh her down like an old, tired coat. Suddenly she wanted to shrug free of the feeling, cast it aside and merely be.

It dawned on her then. She wanted to be like these people. Mrs. Stone looked at her children, not merely with love, but with pride. Pride for who they were, the adults they had become. She wanted, needed, that kind of acceptance. No struggle, no proving herself worthy of love.

That was what she'd done all her life. She'd been too afraid to stray from Walt and Grams, too afraid the bond would be broken by distance, by the separation.

Had her foster parents asked that of her? No, she couldn't say they had. It was something—some fear of her own—that had taken root and sprouted long ago.

Katherine felt a warm, soft hand close around hers, and looked up to find Mrs. Stone smiling at her. "I don't want today to pass without telling you how happy we are to have you here."

"Th-thank you," Katherine stammered, jolted from her thoughts by the older woman's kind words.

"No matter how old your children get, they're still your children." Mrs. Stone removed her hand from Katherine's arm and clasped her hands together. "And no matter how old they get, you still worry."

Aaron's mother looked directly into her eyes, and Katherine sensed her need to continue without interruption.

Mrs. Stone returned her hand to Katherine's arm, and her eyes pooled with tears. "We had begun to wonder, until today, if Aaron would ever get over Jacqueline's suicide."

Jacqueline's suicide. Katherine felt shock waves pulse through her body. *Jacqueline's suicide.* She breathed deeply as her vision blurred. Of course she'd known, hadn't she? She'd dreamed of Jacqueline with startling clarity, undeniable emotion. What she had was a gift, some type of vision. Simple as that. Nothing to be frightened of.

"We never even met her. I guess that was the first time Aaron ever fell in love." Katherine heard Mrs. Stone's voice through a haze of panic. "That's the hardest to get over, you know . . ."

"*Let's leave your mother alone right now, honey.*" Her

father's voice found her, sought her out after all these years—brought with it that horrible day. She hadn't realized, until now, that her father's voice had sounded different. She recognized the difference now, though. He had been afraid.

Afraid of what was happening to her mother.

"But what's wrong with Mommy?" Katherine remembered crying then, and her father had pulled her against him for a rare hug. *"She was talking to Grandma, but Grandma's dead. Isn't she?"*

The hug had ended all too quickly. *"Mommy is sick, honey, that's all."*

Insanity.

Fear clutched at her chest, clawed at her throat and eyes until Katherine was certain she was about to scream with the effort it took to keep the tears at bay.

"Katherine? Oh Katherine, honey, I'm sorry I mentioned it. I assumed that you and Aaron had talked about Jacqueline."

"Yes." Katherine fixed a smile on her face as she shook her head. "No. I mean—it's not a problem." She looked the older woman in the eye and answered her as honestly as she could. "I knew about Jacqueline."

She knew about Jacqueline. She knew about Owen Blake, about Cheryl's pregnancy, David's wife's untimely death. She knew . . . Oh Lord, her abilities had gone from strange coincidence, intuition, to something else. Something that frightened her more than words could say. The image of her mother's tortured, twisted features flashed before her eyes. She had left this world long before her body gave up the fight. Insanity. How ironic it would be if this were the only link she shared with her mother.

"Oh thank heavens." Katherine watched Mrs. Stone, obviously relieved, sink against the back of her chair. "From the expression on your face, I thought I'd spoken out of turn."

Katherine swallowed hard, and tried to rub away the chill bumps that rippled across her upper arms. "No, that's perfectly all right." She had to leave. Now. She needed time alone, time to sort things out. "But I'm afraid I'm not feeling well."

She stood, and the sound of her heavy chair scraping against the concrete set her nerves on end. Her skin felt painfully tight, her chest constricted until the simple act of breathing took all her concentration.

"You sit back down, honey." Mrs. Stone rose from her chair. "I'll get Aaron."

No, she couldn't sit down. She was too afraid she wouldn't be able to stand up again. Forcing air into her lungs, she begged her shaking limbs to cooperate. She desperately wanted to hold on to her dignity, to smile and wave good-bye to Aaron's family—Aaron's nice, normal family—as if nothing were wrong.

She smiled at Faith, then glanced at Mrs. Stone. Aaron's mother's eyes were too probing, too knowing, for Katherine to hold her gaze long. "I didn't get much sleep last night. I don't know if Aaron mentioned it, but my apartment was broken into recently and . . ." She allowed her voice to trail off as she detected a note of hysteria creeping into it. Everything seemed to be happening at double speed. She rubbed her damp palms against her shorts and tried to interject a calm tone to her words. "I haven't been sleeping well since then."

"You poor dear. I didn't know. . . ."

Mrs. Stone's words faded as Katherine's gaze locked with Aaron's. Even from across the lawn, she could see his forehead pucker into a worried frown. He began to walk toward her, his long, easy stride quickly covering the distance that separated them.

"Is something wrong?" He stopped before her, absently shifting a red Frisbee from hand to hand.

Katherine watched the movement of the toy with nauseating intensity. She wanted to scream, wanted to bolt from the probing gazes of Aaron's family.

"I'm not feeling well." Her voice could have been a stranger's. She continued, though, trying in vain to force herself to sound normal. "I think the lack of sleep is finally catching up with me."

Aaron only frowned, his eyes narrowed as he watched her fumble for the right words. She needed him to understand, to take her hand and lead her toward the truck. To take her home. Now. Before she lost control.

Instead he just stared at her, his eyes suspicious, his body unmoving.

Katherine turned and grasped Mrs. Stone's hands. If she didn't get out of there soon, she was going to scream. "I hate to cut the day short, but I'm afraid I need to get some sleep." She nodded in Faith's direction, then looked back at Aaron's mother. "Thank you for having me. Will you tell David and the others that I said good-bye?"

"Of course," Mrs. Stone responded, squeezing her hand. "I hope Aaron will bring you back soon."

"Thank you," Katherine replied, purposely avoiding Aaron's eyes.

"Aaron! Stop standing there like a statue and take hold of Katherine. She's pale as a sheet."

Aaron allowed the Frisbee to drop to the ground, then looped his arm around her shoulders. Together they turned toward the decline that would lead them back to the truck. Back home. Relief flowed through her. Behind her she could hear the others wishing her well, inviting her back. . . . She glanced over her shoulder and smiled, raising her hand in Robert and Raece's direction—a silent good-bye.

If Aaron was worried about her, the speed with which they walked down the gentle hill didn't reflect it. Perhaps he didn't believe her. She wouldn't be surprised. His eyes had held suspicion, his gaze had flowed over her with scrutiny instead of concern.

The truck's engine was still warm, she noticed, as she and Aaron crossed to the passenger door. She wanted to sob with relief as she slipped inside the vehicle, wanted to bury her face as the door closed behind her, shutting out the sights and sounds, the shifting faces of the people she had just left behind. The overwhelming emotion.

Aaron opened the door and slid in beside her. He'd been silent, not offering her sympathy, not asking her any questions. Funny, she thought, how the day had gone from welcoming to suffocating with one word.

Jacqueline.

No. No, she wouldn't allow herself to think about

that right now. She wanted—needed—things to seem normal. *Make-believe*, a voice whispered in her ear. *Normal is only make-believe.*

She silenced the voice. Talk. Aaron was too quiet, his gaze suddenly too keen. Katherine glanced around her, searching for a source of conversation. As before, she noticed the motorcycle parked next to the line of cars, the little pink tricycle resting next to it.

"So which one of the kids hero-worships Raece?" she asked, hoping the nervous trill in her voice wasn't obvious.

Aaron followed her gaze. "Oh, that's Megan's," he answered with a smirk.

Katherine sighed, relieved to see some of the suspicious creases in his face soften. *Hold on*, she told herself. *Keep talking. You'll be home soon.*

"She wants to be just like him," Aaron continued. "Marie and Calvin break out in a cold sweat every time they think about it."

"The rebel of the family?" Somehow she'd known that the motorcycle was Raece's, though she really hadn't cast Raece in the role of rebellious son. In fact, she suspected that Aaron held that position. Whatever the case, she was grateful to have something else to think about, to occupy her thoughts.

"Retired rebel would be more like it." Aaron's smile was even softer this time.

She focused on the image of Raece, welcomed the preoccupation as the trembling of her hands eased. In her mind she saw his gentle way of walking, the lean silhouette of his body. Aaron braked before pulling out onto the highway, jolting her from her thoughts. Once again, the silence in the cab of the truck threatened to suffocate her.

Talk, she reminded herself. *Make everything normal. . . .*

"So has Raece gotten a clean bill of health?" As soon as she uttered the last syllable, she froze. She smothered a small cry of denial as Aaron's gaze snapped in her direction.

What had she just said? Her disjointed thoughts swirled about her. Clean bill of health? No, it couldn't be. She hadn't known. *Just apologize*, she told herself. *Tell him you were thinking of someone else.*

Aaron's brows lowered, and he cocked his head slightly before returning his gaze to the road. "I'm surprised Faith told you. Raece is a really private person." He flexed his fingers against the steering wheel, his body suddenly tense. "He doesn't normally talk about the leukemia."

The cab was spinning. Katherine buried one hand into the plush fabric of the seat; the other grasped the door handle until her fingers ached. The colors—the green of the trees, the yellow and white road markings, the steel-gray of the asphalt—danced and swirled, threatening to meld into a kaleidoscope of panic.

Her throat tightened, sweat beaded on her forehead, then felt uncomfortably cold in the air-conditioned truck. *Oh God, it had happened again.* One hand clutched the base of her throat. Her first instinct was to explain—no—make excuses for why she'd known something she wasn't supposed to know. After all, that's what she'd done all her life.

She was suddenly tired—tired of knowing, tired of

explaining. But she was more afraid of being totally honest with Aaron. *He won't believe you,* a voice whispered. She swallowed down the panic as seconds ticked by like minutes. Of course he wouldn't believe her, so why feed the fires of suspicion? After all, she'd just won some small measure of his trust. She could feel the tension radiating from his body, see the doubt lingering in his gaze.

"Your mother." She forced the words out, surprised that her voice sounded convincingly calm this time.

"What about her?"

"It wasn't Faith who told me about Raece's leukemia, it was your mother."

"Oh," he said, nodding thoughtfully.

Katherine remembered to breathe again. The lie had worked. He hadn't asked any questions. Better still, the telltale creases of suspicion hadn't returned to his eyes. She smiled sincerely in his direction.

When had she decided to lie? Grasping for normalcy with Aaron was, admittedly, pointless. After all, hadn't she already asked him to believe the unbelievable? She straightened her shoulders and tried to shrug off the guilt. It had been the coward's way out, but at least the panic had subsided. She breathed deeply and unclasped her suddenly steady hands. It was better this way. At least for her.

At least for now.

She glanced nervously in Aaron's direction and plunged on, hoping her instincts wouldn't fail her this time. "I hope you're not angry with your mother." He might have chastised Faith for the breach of confidence, but not his mother. And as long as he didn't mention it, the lie would stand.

It had to. Because today a new truth had emerged, one that tangled her up with Aaron Stone in a way she'd never imagined possible, with emotions and desires she'd never known she possessed.

Katherine watched the yellow center line stripes of the road tick by. Everything was in focus again, with consistent rhythm and clarity.

The burden of deceit was heavy, yet comforting. Like an old blanket, she thought. Dirty, but warm all the same. She bit her lower lip in determination, knowing she would find a way to deal with it.

She would deal with it because she couldn't bear to see the suspicion return to Aaron's eyes, couldn't face what that would mean. She refolded her hands in her lap. She would tell Aaron everything one day soon.

When she could find a way to make him believe her.

SEVEN

The knife cut an even slice through the meaty flesh of the eggplant, and Aaron plopped the last of the sliced vegetable into a bowl of salty ice water. He glanced behind him at Katherine, who was quietly—too quietly—spreading butter on a loaf of sourdough bread.

We need to nail down the link between Katherine Jackson and Owen Blake, or we need to dismiss her as a suspect entirely. Aaron winced as he recalled his lieutenant's words. *And I, for one, am not willing to do that. She didn't call the Scenic View Inn and ask for the man for no reason.*

No, she hadn't, Aaron reminded himself. Not unless he was willing to believe she had some kind of psychic ability. Every logical bone in his body told him that was absurd, but the more time he spent with Katherine, the less certain he was about anything.

She had barely said two words to him on the way home from David's house, and he hadn't been able to reach her by phone in the two-day interim since.

He'd finally given up on the telephone, and had

shown up on her doorstep that night with a bottle of zinfandel, roma tomatoes, eggplant, and enough fresh oregano to spice a tubful of eggplant Parmesan. She had seemed genuinely pleased to see him, though more than a little nervous, and had made some flimsy excuse for not returning his calls. In the end, she'd invited him in, and accepted his offer to cook dinner.

Still, something about her smile—or perhaps it was the lingering sadness in her eyes when she smiled—left him aching to discover the source of her pain.

But that was only one of many answers he needed.

His gaze flowed over her, searching for some indication, at least a physical one, that something was wrong. Her hair had been loose when she'd opened the door. He had objected—and had won the battle—when she'd wanted to pull it back as they cooked. Now it swung almost to her hips, covering her shoulders and back in a velvet cascade. He wanted to bury his face in the fragrant silkiness of it, to press his body against her back, feel the womanly softness of her buttocks in contrast to his hardness.

She chose to turn and look at him at that moment. Her face looked flushed, her expression slightly embarrassed. Had she read his thoughts? Aaron plunged his hands into the ice water and began to transfer the slices of eggplant into a second bowl.

Business was getting tangled up with pleasure lately, and that was something he never allowed to happen. Or at least he hadn't allowed it to happen since Jacqueline's death. In his mind he saw the tangled metal that had been her car, the severed utility pole, with its upper half swinging like a macabre pendulum above it. Time. He should have given her time. The pressure had been too much, and she'd responded to his ultimatum by ending her life.

Aaron felt his chest ache, and realized he was holding his breath. He breathed in deep then, wanting to abolish the horrible image from his mind. Maybe if Jacqueline hadn't chosen such a violent way to leave this world . . . But then again, that was all she'd known. Maybe, to her, slamming her car into a utility pole at breakneck speed hadn't seemed violent compared to the hell she lived in every day.

Forget it, he told himself. How many hours had he walked the two-lane road where the accident had occurred, both in reality and in his mind? How many times had he tried to fabricate a reason for the accident? The other officers had assumed suicide the moment they arrived at the scene. There was no rain, no ice, no other vehicle to blame for the collision. Just Jacqueline's car and a telephone pole thick enough to stop a freight train dead in its tracks. He shook his head to clear the image. He'd known the truth, he just hadn't wanted to face it. Hell, he still didn't want to face his part in it.

When he felt Katherine's gaze on him again, he realized he was standing, his fingers curled around a handful of wet eggplant, staring out the kitchen window. He allowed the fragrant slices of vegetable to drop into the second bowl and plastered a smile on his face.

"Daydreaming?" she asked.

"Mm. Dreaming in any context seems to be a sore subject around here. Maybe I should take the Fifth."

She smiled, and this time the smile actually reached her eyes. "Maybe you should."

"You know what's wrong here?" he asked.

She shook her head.

"You're cooking."

"So?"

"When I offered to cook you dinner, that's what I meant." He moved past her and pulled the bottle of wine from a large glass mixing bowl filled with ice. He uncorked it and poured an amount that would have given Emily Post the vapors. Pushing the glass into her hand, he pointed toward the sofa. "Take this and go sit down."

She stared at the glass. "I don't drink."

"Wait a minute." He poured a second glass for himself. "I thought you meant you didn't drink hard liquor."

She sniffed the liquid as if she were determining whether or not it was poison. "There's a difference?"

He stifled a laugh. "Yes, there's a difference." He didn't know whether to nominate her for an Academy Award or arrest her for taking the innocent charade too far. "This is just wine. Besides, you can't have my eggplant Parmesan without a glass of zinfandel."

She took a hesitant sip, then nodded. "It's good." She smiled a mischievous smile that shot him through the heart and warmed his body at the same time. "I'll make a deal with you. I'll try the wine if you'll let me stay in the kitchen."

He straightened, realizing that he'd started leaning toward her. God, he wanted to kiss her. So what was stopping him? Something in her posture, in her eyes.

He couldn't put his finger on it, but since they'd returned from David's, she'd acted as if she were hiding something. At least, that's what his gut was telling him.

At that moment he wanted his instincts to shut up—at least the professional ones. She ran her tongue over her lips, and he knew the light taste of wine would be lingering on them. He wanted this woman, wanted to taste her lips, feel her body. . . .

But for now he'd settle for looking at her. "I have an even better deal."

She looked suspicious. "Which is . . . ?"

"You go put on one of the dresses you made, and you can do anything you want."

He watched as she took another sip of wine. A rather large sip, he noted.

"Something so beautiful wasn't meant to be hidden away," he added. Light danced in her eyes, but he couldn't tell if it was appreciation or wariness.

"I could point out," she said, "that since this is my apartment, I can do anything I please." Another sip—no gulp—of wine went down. "But I have a counteroffer. I'll go put on one of the dresses if you'll hear me out about the dream—"

She threw up her hand as he started to protest, then took advantage of the pause by sipping more wine.

She swallowed. "Will you promise to listen with an open mind this time?"

He nodded. "Deal."

"Okay, then." She pulled the bottle of wine out of the mixing bowl and refilled her glass. "I'll be right back."

Aaron started to comment on the speed with which

she'd consumed the first glass, but bit his tongue. She wasn't acting like someone who had never had wine. "Katherine—"

She turned. "Yes?"

"Wear the black one." He gestured with his hands. "The one with the white collar and the black beads."

A soft smile crossed her lips, one he doubted that she meant to be seductive, but was all the same. She nodded. "Okay."

Aaron watched her go, then busied himself—busied his mind—with the task of coating the eggplant in the bread crumb mixture. . . . *She didn't call the Scenic View Inn and ask for the man for no reason.* The lieutenant's words taunted him as he lowered the slices into the sizzling oil.

Was he even capable of believing Katherine's explanation?

He lifted the lid to the pot where the tomato sauce was bubbling, and the fragrant smell of garlic, tomatoes, and oregano soothed him. Abilities. He'd heard other cops, ones who had transferred from other districts, talk about using psychics in unsolved cases. To his knowledge, though, his department had never even dabbled in anything like that. But if other people, other professionals, were willing to believe in such things . . .

Aaron stirred the tomato sauce, tasted it, then added more crushed oregano. He drank the last of his wine as he stared at the hypnotic motion of the boiling mixture, trying to consider the possibility with an open mind. Okay—so on occasion he'd reached for the phone just before it rang. Weird. But that was hardly psychic ability. Or was it? He rubbed his forehead in frustration.

He did have to admit to one thing, though. He'd used hunches to solve cases. How many times had he followed a lead that wasn't a lead at all, but a gut instinct instead? Maybe whatever ability Katherine possessed wasn't far from the same thing. In that case, it would be as innocent as it was unbelievable.

He slapped the lid back over the simmering sauce and looked around him. Roscoe was asleep on his sheepskin rug in the next room, Katherine's jungle of houseplants were contentedly tangling themselves around any piece of furniture or doodad that was stationary, and the apartment was filled with the homey scent of buttered bread and Italian spices. Aaron noticed two fat, previously lit candles in terra-cotta pots on the kitchen table. He pulled his lighter from his jeans' pocket—the only thing about smoking that he'd discovered to be a good idea—lit the two candles, and switched off the dining room light.

At first glance everything seemed so peaceful. Perfect, in fact. But, in truth, everything was a shambles.

Loyalty, instinct, suspicion, and—lately—more dangerous emotions were becoming tangled in a web of confusion. His mind paused to examine his reasons for being with Katherine that night, but he pushed the question aside. Duty, desire—what did it matter? The more time he spent with her, the better. Whether it was for professional or purely personal reasons, was beside the point. The end result would be the same. He was determined to gather enough facts to either dismiss her as a suspect or make her the focus of the investigation.

The sound of rustling material jerked his head up. Katherine stood before him in the hallway, the black velvet evening gown draped around her tall frame in sheer perfection. All other thoughts were immediately blotted from his mind by the shimmering vision. She'd coiled her thick hair atop her head, and the white satin collar that topped the black velvet just skimmed her upper arms, leaving her shoulders, as well as a large expanse of creamy white chest, bare.

His breath caught in his throat, and his body reacted immediately to the sight of her, and to the rather uninhibited look in her eyes. He noticed the empty glass that dangled from one hand, and wondered how much of her sultry expression could be attributed to the wine.

You still don't know who killed Owen Blake, a voice—the voice of reason—whispered in his ear. *You still don't know who might be involved.*

"You lit the candles." She smiled as she walked toward the table, running her fingers over the wood.

He nodded. "The dress is beautiful." His voice sounded husky, but he was proud of himself for stopping short of telling her how gorgeous she looked. Desire was pelting him like warm rain, but he couldn't—shouldn't—let Katherine know.

Still his body ached for hers, his arms longed to hold her. If the circumstances were different, if she weren't technically still a suspect, would he feel the same? He hadn't found the courage in the ten years since Jacqueline's death to care for anyone, but somehow Katherine was different.

Reserve judgment. Wait and see what she might reveal.

Candlelight sparkled in her innocent green eyes, a paradox to the luscious body she possessed. And to his own suspicion, Aaron realized. He shifted uncomfortably. Mixing business and pleasure didn't suit him.

Katherine hadn't put on any shoes, hadn't known what to do, actually. At least five minutes had passed as she'd stood in the sewing room, staring at her bare feet and wondering what to do. Bare feet looked ridiculous, but she didn't own any high heels. And why would she, since she'd never planned on allowing anyone to see the gowns, much less model them for anyone? You didn't tend shop in heels, for heaven's sake. The fact that the gowns were tailored to fit her body was simply a matter of convenience. There wasn't anyone else around to use as a model.

In the end, she'd downed the last of the wine, gathered her courage, and walked barefoot back down the hall. But now a new fear was gnawing at her, and it had everything to do with the look in Aaron's eyes. He wanted to make love to her. He didn't necessarily care for her—probably didn't even believe her. But he wanted her.

And heaven help her, she wanted him too.

Was she ready to damn the circumstances, damn the truth? Yes, part of her was. But another part refused to let it go, ached with the need to have Aaron believe her, longed to trust him with the truth. The truth about Jacqueline.

"You look beautiful." Aaron suddenly appeared uncomfortable as he said the words. He turned his back to her and resumed the task of cooking.

She followed him, her body returning the unspoken

desire that radiated from his, her mind jumbled with emotions that she dared not recognize. She stopped just short of reaching out, her fingers curling into a fist in an effort not to touch him.

She was tired of pretending. She thought back on the easy way Aaron's family spent time with one another. No secrets, no holding back. Somehow, with Walt and Grams, she'd held a part of herself back. It had been unintentional, so subtle, she hadn't even realized she'd been doing it. But it had happened. She loved them unconditionally, but was too afraid to trust in their unconditional love. Now she realized that she'd not only cheated herself, she'd cheated them.

Acceptance. How sweet it would be to be accepted for simply who she was. She recalled the absolute love she'd seen in Aaron's mother's eyes. She ached for that. She'd ached for that all her life. A painful emptiness revealed itself with that realization, and she crossed her arms over her chest in an attempt to ward off a sudden chill.

"My birth mother was insane," she blurted out. "But I guess you knew that." She knew the words sounded stark, unexpected. Maybe it was the wine. In any case, it was too late to take them back.

Aaron's brow puckered, but he never stopped tending the slices of frying eggplant. Finally he looked over his shoulder to meet her eyes. "I knew from the background check that she died when you were eight, but—"

"It's taken me years to come to terms with it, to say the words 'mentally ill.' " She moved to stand next to him, feeling as if she'd unburdened part of the load.

Unfortunately there was more. There was Jacqueline.

"What do you need, a glass oven dish maybe?"

Aaron looked surprised, and Katherine realized she'd abruptly started talking about something else. She did feel talkative, less nervous. Maybe it was the wine. It was good, but it was making her mouth dry. She crossed to the bottle and sloshed a little more into her empty glass, drank it, then began to riffle around in the cabinet.

"Ta-da," she said as she emerged with the dish.

"Uh . . . thanks."

Aaron frowned at her as he ladled sauce into the dish. Why was he frowning? She was actually beginning to enjoy herself. There was a gorgeous man in her kitchen cooking her dinner, and looking at her as though she were the main course.

She thought she'd feel ridiculous walking around in her kitchen in the evening gown, but instead she felt surprisingly at home in it, and proud of the way it flattered her body. It was elegant, and for the first time in her life, she felt elegant too. She'd lovingly put in every stitch, tacked each and every bead in place, and painstakingly planned the drape of the fabric, yet she was amazed that it had actually worked, that it had come together to become something beautiful.

She smiled. Aaron had actually called the gown her "creation."

She watched as he confidently arranged the layers of sauce, cheese, and eggplant in the glass dish, then slid it into the warm oven. Everything about him fascinated her. The aura of mystery and suspicion was still a constant backdrop to the odd intimacy they shared. Suddenly she wanted this night and everything it had to offer, wanted to forget her problems, to shed her inadequacies—her inhibitions.

Hadn't she spent her share of lonely evenings at home, conjuring up such a fantasy? The idea that Aaron was another one of her images sent a manic laugh bubbling from her before she could clasp her hand over her mouth.

"What's so funny?" He glanced at her wineglass as a reserved grin tugged at the corners of his mouth.

"You." She shook her head as her fingertips brushed his upper arm. "I was just wondering if you're for real or if I conjured you up along with Owen Blake."

He caught her wrist, his grip almost painfully tight. His eyes were lit with something she didn't understand, until his gaze flickered over her body, lingering on her breasts. Desire, hot and dangerous, oozed from him. She wanted to run, yet she wanted to stay—to press her body against his, feel his arousal nestled against her hips.

His arousal . . . She realized, then, that she wasn't merely assuming the way Aaron felt, but she knew. She knew. Her head swam with the realization. His thoughts were becoming tangled with hers.

Her own desire coiled within her, and her breath caught sharply at the feel of his fingers stroking the skin of her wrist. What would it be like to be touched—completely touched—by Aaron? He reached out with his free hand and removed the glass from her fingers.

Something other than passion lingered in his eyes, and she recognized the white-hot light as anger. But why would he be angry with her? The thought barely had time to register before his mouth found hers. His kiss wasn't angry, it was sexual. There was simply no other word for it. The expert thrust of his tongue was masculine, and her mouth accepted his—willing and female. She felt her muscles weaken and her body slide against his.

His mouth trailed kisses to her ear. "I'm real," he whispered.

His body was a fascinating mixture of soft skin and hard muscle, she realized as she felt her breasts crushed against the flat planes of his chest. Her fingers found the loose material of his shirt, and she pulled it from the waistband of his jeans so that she could slide her hands against his hot flesh. He moaned as she dug her fingers into his thick chest hair and gently raked her fingernails across his hardened nipple. She loved the way her touch excited him. It was a new feeling, one of power, she realized. Confidence was a delicious sensation she never knew she possessed.

"I want you," he whispered, his mouth still pressed against her neck. "So tell me no."

Her hands stilled as she tried to make sense of his words. Was he going to tell her he was still in love with Jacqueline's memory? She didn't dare meet his eyes, didn't have the courage. Instead she pressed her cheek against his chest. "Why?" she finally asked.

"Because I don't want you only once." His voice was husky, vibrating against her ear. His hands moved to find her breasts, then sought out her nipples, pressing them firmly between his fingers and the material of the gown. "So if there's something I should know, tell me now. Tell me while I can still stop what we're about to do."

The pounding of her pulse almost drowned out his words, and the feel of his fingers as they caressed her nipples hazed her vision. "I don't want to stop what we're about to do." She pulled back slightly to meet his eyes. "And I didn't kill Owen Blake, if that's what you need to hear—"

"The last thing I want to think about is Owen Blake."

Aaron moved into action as he uttered the last words. He gently pushed the neckline of her gown down, freeing one breast. Katherine heard the sharp intake of her own breath, as his hands circled her heavy breast and lifted it to his lips. Hot and slick, his mouth closed over her bare nipple and suckled, sending a wave of desire flowing from his mouth to the very core of her womanhood. Her fingers tangled in his hair, urging him closer, to continue.

Then he stopped.

Slowly, with excruciating tenderness, he eased the gown back over her breast, its satin neckline disguising the passion that passed between them. Katherine stifled a cry of denial. Had he changed his mind? Then he reached for her hand, entwining his warm fingers with hers, and tugged her down the hall toward her bedroom. She understood then, and her heart leaped. He didn't want to take her for the first time, however willing she was, without ceremony—without the respect she deserved.

She followed him through the bedroom doorway, then stopped as he hesitated. He turned toward her, his expression revealing his need.

"Are you certain?" he asked, stroking her cheek.

She nodded. "Yes."

He turned her back to him and unzipped the gown with one motion. She started to face him again, but he stopped her with a firm hand to her shoulder. Instinctively, she hesitated as he slipped his hands beneath the fabric that covered her shoulders and eased the gown from her arms, then pushed it, along with her panties, past her hips.

Any other time, with any other man, she would have felt vulnerable. But not this time, not with Aaron. She could feel the light movement of air as he unbuttoned his shirt and slid it off, but nothing could prepare her for the sensual feel of his flesh as he brushed his chest against her back. Hot. His skin was hot against hers, and she could just make out the masculine feel of his chest hair as he slid his upper body against hers.

All too soon he stepped away, but she didn't dare move. She could hear the rustle of fabric as he stepped out of his jeans. Katherine held her breath. It was cold without his touch, and she wanted to feel him. . . .

Spots of light danced before her eyes as his body found hers again. She felt the warmth of his thighs before his erection touched her buttocks, then probed gently between her legs.

He made a low groan of satisfaction, but held perfectly still. It seemed they stood that way for eternity before he moved again, sliding flesh against flesh without entering her—denying her the one thing her body ached for.

Instead he withdrew to plant light kisses along her side. But when she made a move to turn toward him, the kisses went from gentle to commanding, and traveled from the innocent flesh of her side to the intimate, sensitive skin of her nipples.

"Aaron . . ."

He pressed his finger against her lips. "Shh," he soothed. His fingertip probed gently then, entering her mouth with a lover's curiosity. Instinctively she found his finger with her tongue and drew it farther into her mouth.

The simple motion seemed to be Aaron's undoing. She felt his erection grow even harder against her upper thighs before he scooped her up into his arms. In a flash she was on the bed, with Aaron warm and ready between her legs. Only then did she realize he'd already protected her. The thought lingered for just a moment as her gaze took in the full size of him. He ran his hands up the length of her legs, easing her thighs farther apart until the tip of him was nestled against her.

Her body was ready for him. She could feel the warm moisture welcoming him as he pushed carefully into her. A small cry of surprise escaped her as he entered her fully, but his mouth silenced her with a kiss. Her body relaxed beneath his as he made love to her mouth with his tongue.

He began to move inside her then too, and the raw pleasure almost pulled her over the edge. Too soon, she thought.

"Wait . . ." she whispered.

He pushed fully into her before hesitating. Instead of easing her desire, though, the sensation of being completely filled by Aaron only intensified her need.

She clasped his back, fingers pressing into his flesh, urging, begging him without words to continue. He moved again, sensing her readiness, and the pleasure was even sweeter. He lowered his chest to hers, and the sweat-slicked skin of their bodies mated in silence.

She wanted the feeling to last forever, but her body plunged ahead, greedily drawing Aaron fully into her as he thrust. She relished in the pleasure, the musky scent of warmed skin. As his mouth found hers again, her senses took in the light taste of the wine—and the more heady masculine taste of Aaron—and she knew she couldn't wait any longer.

"Aaron . . ."

He pressed his finger against her lips again, and again she sucked on it. She felt him grow within her. Once, twice, three times he thrust inside her before she couldn't hold on to the pleasure any longer. Together their bodies tightened against each other and together they found their release.

The silence that followed wasn't awkward. Instead it was as comfortable as the silence of their lovemaking. Katherine curled against Aaron as he gently pulled free from her body and rolled them to their sides.

He nuzzled the back of her neck. "Hungry?"

The sumptuous smell of the baking eggplant Parmesan registered abruptly. A sharp rumble of hunger in her stomach followed as the aroma drifted into the bedroom.

"Uh-huh," she replied. One hunger had been satisfied, but a simpler one still called. She snuggled against Aaron for a moment, enjoying their closeness. "Do you think it's done yet?"

He laughed, and the throaty sound sent new shivers of awareness down her spine. "I have no idea. I've lost all track of time. But I'm willing to go investigate if you are."

"Ready and willing." She planted a quick kiss on his lips before sliding from the bed. The truth was, she wanted to stay in his arms, wanted to clutch the feeling to her for dear life. She wanted the moment to last forever, but that thought was way too dangerous. The safest thing to do was to keep moving, to not let herself think of possibilities that might never be.

As she found her robe, she watched Aaron step back into his briefs and jeans. When she'd first been the object of his suspicious scowl, she would never have dreamed that they could become lovers, much less feel so totally at ease with each other. He crossed the room to take her hand, and together they strolled back to the kitchen.

After they had finished most of the eggplant Parmesan and drained the last drop of the wine, Katherine leaned across the kitchen table to take Aaron's hand. "You know you didn't keep up your end of the bargain."

He looked surprised, then smiled a mischievous smile. "I thought I did."

She didn't return his smile. The truth was too important to her. "You know that's not what I meant. You promised to listen to me about the dream with an open mind, remember?"

"Let's not talk about it tonight." There was a wicked light in his eyes as he met her gaze. "How about first thing in the morning?"

A spark of hope was lit within her at his words. He was asking to stay the night. And she wanted him to, wanted it more than anything she could remember wanting—or needing—in a long time. Yet part of her wanted to insist that he hear her out about the dream. She wasn't prepared to tell him about Jacqueline, or even that she'd sensed Raece's illness rather than being told about it, but she needed to make him understand how she'd known about Owen Blake. Prove her innocence. It was the first difficult, but necessary, step.

Sooner or later, though, it would include being honest about Jacqueline as well. But how far could she push him, how much could she expect him to believe? Katherine swallowed hard, as her fear of losing Aaron battled with her need to make him understand her. She felt her courage wither and die as she hesitated. Was it so wrong to want to hold on to the moment, to savor the happiness she and Aaron had shared tonight . . . if only for a little while longer?

"In the morning," she said finally. "Promise?"

He ran his fingertips over her knuckles. "Promise."

Together they made their way back down the hall and crawled beneath the covers with the ease of lovers who had been with each other for years. It was easy to pretend that the suspicion and deceit had never existed as Aaron pulled her against his hard body, and settled his chin against the curve of her neck.

Katherine closed her eyes. It wouldn't hurt to pretend. Would it?

"Please let me take care of you. Please, Jacqueline."

Aaron's words had echoed in her head all night, tempting her. To allow herself to believe in the future was dangerous. She dabbed makeup on her bruised cheekbone, then wiped away a tear that threatened to undo her pitiful attempts at masking the dark purple mark.

Could she go to him? Did she dare? He had the protection of the police force, after all. But would that be enough to keep him safe? In her mind she could see the sincerity, the determination and strength in his eyes. Jacqueline met her own eyes in the mirror, and struggled to find the person she had once been. She remembered the laughing brown eyes of a child, but the eyes that stared back at her were dull, lifeless . . . old.

But still there was a spark of hope that refused to die. She couldn't see it, but she could feel it if she concentrated . . . if she dared to let herself hope. Suddenly it started to grow, taking root and opening up to possibilities.

She would go to him, accept his help, if not his love. He thought he was in love with her. She knew that. But in her heart she knew it was his desire to help her, to save her, that fueled his emotions. She couldn't return his love. No, she wasn't certain she was even capable of loving again. At least not in that way.

But Aaron would help her, and she would go to him. Today. Right now. Tears threatened to spill again as she thought of how sweet it would be to rest her head against his strong shoulder, to feel secure once more.

And maybe, in time, she could learn to love again.

Jacqueline parted the curtains of the trailer and looked outside. The beat-up old Volkswagen looked like heaven to her. Grasping the keys in her hand, she dashed out the door, stumbling over the trailer's cinder-block stairs, and ran toward the car.

Freedom. It soared within her, blocking out the fear. She turned the key in the ignition and sent up a prayer of thanks as the little engine purred with life.

Today she would leave the ugliness behind, today she would find a new beginning. Today she would go to Aaron.

Warm fingers stroked her face, a voice whispered soothing words. No, she couldn't listen. She had to get away. Now, before it was too late. Before *he* came back to hurt her again. Aaron would be waiting for her. . . .

"Katherine." The voice came to her again, penetrating the haze of sleep. "Katherine, it's okay. You're dreaming."

She sat upright in bed, clutching the sweat-dampened sheet to her chest. Her fingers ached as she squeezed the material in her fists, and her pulse pounded painfully at her temples. She turned her head slightly to find Aaron. His face was barely visible in the near-darkness of the room, but the look of concern was evident nonetheless.

He reached for her hand. "You were having a nightmare."

A nightmare. He was right, of course. It was all a nightmare. But instead of dreaming, she had experienced another vision of Jacqueline. There was no denying it. For some reason she had become privy to the emotions Jacqueline had experienced before her death, whether she wanted to or not.

Her gaze scanned the body of the man who lay next to her. Aaron. She couldn't explain it, didn't have the courage to try to analyze it, but somehow the visions were connected to him.

But this time she'd learned something new. Jacqueline had decided to go to Aaron after all. So what had happened? Aaron's mother had said she committed suicide, but in the dream Jacqueline was going to Aaron. What had changed her mind? Katherine cradled her head in her hands. The thoughts, the emotions, were too much. She felt as if she were losing her mind.

Mommy is sick, honey.

Please, God, she prayed. *Don't let me end up like my mother.*

"Are you all right?" Aaron slipped his arm around her shoulders, but it was too late. The tears had started to flow, and the release was too welcome to stop.

"No," she whispered into the blanket of darkness that shielded her expression from Aaron's gaze.

She swallowed, determined her voice wouldn't fail her. She couldn't hold the truth back any longer. She had to tell Aaron about Jacqueline. If not for his sake, then for her own sanity. The words had to be formed, had to be clear . . . had to make sense. She had to make him understand.

He caught her face between his large hands. "Tell me," he whispered. "What's wrong?"

She shook her head, willing away the fear that threatened to silence her. "I have to tell you something." She wrapped her fingers around his wrists and pulled his hands away from her face. His fingers were too warm, his touch too comforting. She needed, instead, to find some distance.

Distance was safe. Because Aaron wasn't likely to believe what she was about to say. She wiped the tears from her cheeks. She would say it all the same. She had to. Her knowledge of Owen Blake, of Aaron and Jacqueline, were part of one truth that couldn't be separated and fed to him piece by palatable piece. From this point forward she was going to be accepted for who she was and what she was capable of. Or not accepted at all.

Hysteria threatened to overwhelm her. She could lose everything in the next few minutes, with the next words she would utter. She could lose Aaron . . . her freedom . . . her future.

"I've been dreaming of Jacqueline," she said, her voice a monotone, her emotions temporarily shoved into a safe corner of her mind. "Almost all along. I didn't understand it at first." She stifled a hysterical laugh. "I still don't understand it, but I've been dreaming Jacqueline's thoughts, her emotions . . . the feelings she had for you."

Aaron didn't move for a moment, didn't react at all. Then he slipped from the bed and began to dress. Katherine watched him move about the room, terror threatening to overtake her. He was leaving. Hadn't she known he would?

He pulled his shirt on, buttoned it, and tucked it into his jeans. She could barely make out the expression on his face as muted moonlight lit the room. "So you know about Jacqueline." He shrugged. "I guess I knew that."

A sad acceptance crept into her bones as she realized what he meant. "But you don't believe I *dreamed* about Jacqueline, do you?"

"What did you expect to gain by telling me this? If you had been *dreaming* about Jacqueline all along, why wait until now to tell me?"

Katherine tried to gather her thoughts, to find a way to explain something she could barely explain to herself. "It's complicated . . . I can't pretend any longer. And you need to know the truth."

"So now I do." He walked toward the bedroom door, and Katherine felt a sudden coldness. She was alone again, the bed so cold and empty. Why did she feel as if she'd betrayed his trust, intruded on his privacy? She clamped her hand over her mouth to keep from screaming. She hadn't done anything wrong.

"Aaron—"

"I need to know where you'll be tomorrow."

She felt the fine hairs on the back of her neck rise, and a fresh swell of anger replaced the confusion and guilt. "Is that a professional question or a personal one?"

"Well, since you're so fond of the truth . . ." He placed his hands on his hips and looked away. He paused before speaking, and when he did his voice was a mere whisper. "The truth is, I don't know."

The words hung in the air as he turned and walked from the room. Katherine listened to the steady sound of his footsteps as he strode down the hall, then flinched at the resounding thud of the door as it slammed behind him.

EIGHT

Katherine ripped the heavy tape from the cardboard box and stared at the contents inside. Peppermint oil, bayberry bark, and quassia chips, none of which needed to be stocked. She lined through the listing on the inventory sheet, resealed the box, and carried it to the storage room.

Grams had called from Virginia that morning, and Katherine purposely avoided telling her she'd opened the shop. Hardly anyone had come in, and more than once she'd questioned the wisdom of the choice herself. Still, she had enough on her hands without being chastised by Grams.

And, of course, her troubles were the reason she'd opened the shop in the first place. She loved working there, enjoyed helping others. Through the shop, and through Grams, she'd witnessed the healing power of nature. That brought her immense satisfaction. Katherine froze, the box still in her arms. There was that word again—satisfaction.

The idea of being merely satisfied with life hadn't bothered her until recently. Until she'd met Aaron. She set the cumbersome box on the floor and sat down on top of it. Okay, so there were a few doors she hadn't allowed herself to open, a few opportunities she hadn't considered. But what would she do differently if given the chance to rewrite her life thus far? Probably nothing. She couldn't imagine her life without Walt and Grams in it, couldn't imagine loving anything more than working at the shop.

Admittedly, though, she was guilty of one thing: She had wanted her life, the security she'd found with Walt and Grams, to stay the same. Now she knew it wouldn't. She'd gone from boredom to being a murder suspect in the span of one morning. No, there were no guarantees in life. She may have let the cards fall into place in the past, but from now on she was going to have to make her own tomorrows. For better or for worse.

An image of Aaron stretched lazily across her bed flashed in her mind. She willed it away. All her troubles weren't going to be instantly solved, no matter how determined she was. Keep busy. That was all she could do. She flipped her heavy ponytail over one shoulder, hoisted the box to its proper place on a shelf, and dusted off her hands. Now if she could only arrange her life—her feelings for Aaron—as easily.

A week ago she would have laughed at the possibility of being a murder suspect, but today it loomed all too real. Every time she stopped to consider the situation from Aaron's point of view, she became terrified.

He had every right to believe that she was involved in Owen Blake's murder. In fact, he had no reason not to.

The front doorbell rang like the answer to a prayer, giving her something to concentrate on other than Aaron. She looked up to find Donna Walker, one of her regular customers, enter with Cheryl a few steps behind her. She waved to both women, and waited as Cheryl made her way to the counter.

"Hey, kiddo." Cheryl's smiling face was a welcome reprieve from her dark thoughts.

"Hey, yourself." Katherine pointed toward Cheryl's midsection. "Let's see that silhouette."

Cheryl turned and proudly smoothed her shirt against her belly. Katherine failed to see any change in her friend's paper-thin silhouette, but didn't have the heart to tell her so. With Cheryl's tiny frame, her pregnancy would be evident soon enough.

"You're coming along," Katherine said. "Are you feeling okay?"

"Right as rain." Cheryl cocked her head and studied Katherine's face. "But you don't look so hot. Are you staring at the ceiling again?"

"Staring at the ceiling" was Cheryl's very apt term for Katherine's insomnia, and since there was some truth to the statement, Katherine agreed. "Afraid so."

Donna joined them at the counter, carrying her usual bottle of vitamins, plus a basket full of antiaging supplements and creams.

"Whoa, girl," Cheryl exclaimed. "You've got enough collagen and fruit acid there to smooth the wrinkles out of a rhino!"

Donna placed her hands on her ample hips and

glared at Cheryl. "Honestly, Cheryl, did you get out of line when God passed out tact?"

The two women had known each other since grade school, but Katherine decided it wouldn't hurt to step in.

"You know I can't really recommend most of the antiaging products we stock, Donna." She smiled despite the other woman's frown, trying to lighten up the conversation. "In fact, if not for Gloria Florence, we probably wouldn't bother. She insists that Grams keep stocking it, so we keep a few extra on the shelves to make it worth our while."

A stricken expression crossed Donna's face, and Katherine thought she saw tears pool in the other woman's eyes before she began riffling in her purse. Katherine cast a worried look at Cheryl as a sick feeling crept into the pit of her stomach.

Gloria Florence had an obsession with looking young. Gloria Florence had a thing for men. Oh Lord, she'd done it again.

Cheryl threw back her head and laughed. "Gloria's something, isn't she?" She pulled the skin of her face back toward her ears. "With all the face-lifts she's had, it's a wonder she can still blink. Heck, she probably has her driver's license photo retouched."

But when Donna looked up, she wasn't laughing. Tears flowed down her cheeks in silent streams. She didn't acknowledge them, but in a calm voice said, "Something must be working. Bill's having an affair with her."

"He is not!" Cheryl was at Donna's side in a flash and caught her up in a hug. She stood the other woman away from her and looked directly into her eyes. “Donna, I’ve known Bill as long as I’ve known you. He wouldn’t!”

Donna wiped her cheeks with the back of her hand. “Maybe not, but he wants to. He can’t keep his eyes off her.”

Cheryl winked at Katherine over Donna’s shoulder. “Honey,” she said in her most exaggerated Southern drawl, “he’s probably just wondering where she tucks all that skin.”

At that, the three women burst out laughing. Katherine decided, as she wiped tears of mirth from the corners of her eyes, that she definitely needed to spend more time with Cheryl. Close friendships were something she’d denied herself over the years. Looking back on it, it was easy to see why. She’d been so focused on her relationship with Grams and Walt that she’d kept everyone else at arm’s length.

“Why don’t you go on over to the diner and get James to pour you a cup of coffee?” Cheryl guided Donna toward the door. “I’ll be right over, and we can talk.”

Donna cast a worried glance at the basket of creams and pills still sitting on the countertop. Katherine waved her hand in the air. “Don’t worry—I’ll put them back. Or better yet, I’ll hide them and watch Gloria go into a frenzy.”

As Donna smiled and headed for the door, Cheryl walked back to Katherine. “You drew that out of her in a hurry,” she commented as the door closed behind Donna. “How did you know?”

How did she know? That was a good question. In

fact, she didn't know—not consciously. Whenever she stopped to analyze it, she could see the pattern, could recall the mist of "knowing" that swirled about in the back of her brain, but never really came to the forefront. Until, that is, she had put her foot in her mouth or caused a customer to leave the store in a huff, thoroughly annoyed at her for sticking her nose into their business.

Or called a hotel and asked to speak to a dead drug dealer . . .

Katherine took a steadying breath as a stab of regret hit her. Why had she told Aaron about Jacqueline? The night had been so wonderful, their lovemaking so perfect.

She met Cheryl's gaze. "What would you say if I told you I was psychic?"

Cheryl's eyes widened, but then she merely smiled and shrugged. "Cool."

"Cool?" Katherine repeated. "That's all you have to say?"

"I'd say it would explain a lot." Cheryl pressed her hand to her abdomen. "Is that how you knew about the baby?"

Katherine nodded. "I'm not sure I can explain it, but I seem to have some kind of sixth sense." She frowned. "It's more like a heightened intuition."

"Cool," Cheryl repeated.

Katherine crossed her arms over her chest and studied her friend. Cheryl had accepted the idea without blinking. Cool, indeed. If only Aaron felt the same way.

"Now I have a question." Cheryl leaned against the

counter, a serious expression on her normally cheerful face. "Is everything all right with you—with the shop?"

"Yes." Katherine answered automatically, her first instinct to reassure her friend. Then she caught herself in the lie. "No . . . Well, it's a long story. The duplex was broken into but everything is going to be okay." She smiled at Cheryl, mentally pleading with her to accept the answer at face value. "What made you ask?"

"Oh, thank heavens." Cheryl tucked a lock of auburn hair behind her ear. "James caught someone nosing around in the alley between the diner and the shop. And you know how James can be—I think he scared the life out of the little guy. Turns out, though, that he was a cop. According to James, he asked all sorts of nosy questions about you, about the shop."

Katherine hoped the disappointment she felt didn't show on her face, but she was certain that it did. "When was this?"

"Late yesterday evening."

Her heart felt heavy, as if it took more strength than she had to pump her blood through her body—blood that had suddenly grown cold. She ran her hands up and down her arms. Late yesterday evening Aaron had arrived on her doorstep with a bottle of wine, and they'd made love. . . .

Late yesterday evening, though, she had apparently still been a suspect.

Exhaustion seeped into every bone in her body, and it took all her effort to form a normal expression. "Thanks for letting me know. I'm sure it's nothing." She pretended to arrange the stack of inventory sheets on the counter as she gathered her thoughts. "Listen,

I'm about to close up, and you'd better get back to the diner or Donna may decide to go throttle Bill for something he didn't do."

Cheryl reached out and stilled Katherine's hands, forcing her to lay the inventory sheets down. "Are you sure you're okay?"

"I'm fine, really. I could just use some sleep."

"Okay, but I'm a telephone call away if you need me. You hear?"

Katherine nodded, more grateful for Cheryl's friendship than she could possibly express. At least one person believed in her.

Even if it wasn't the one person she most needed to believe in her.

Aaron picked up the phone, then set it back down in its cradle. He lifted his car keys from the kitchen table, but only twirled them on his finger as he paced the apartment. Dammit, he'd been over the facts a thousand times in his head, and none of it made any sense.

He believed Katherine's story.

He walked to the refrigerator and opened the door, his gaze flowing without interest over the contents inside. He was hungry, but nothing appealed to him. That's how it had been all day. He wanted—needed—to work, but all he'd ended up doing was taking Jacobs's head off. He'd tried to have patience with the rookie, but the kid's incessant enthusiasm for the Blake case was wearing on him. Had forensics determined the exact time of death? Were there any new leads in Katherine's break-in? Aaron couldn't answer Jacobs's questions. He didn't have answers.

Before long, word of his less-than-cheerful mood had spread and everyone at the station was avoiding him. That's when he'd made an excuse about fieldwork, left the station, and ended up at home—pacing.

So much for a change of scenery being the answer. Now the four walls of his apartment were closing in on him. Like a house of cards, he thought bitterly. Damn, but he needed a break in the case. His body warmed when he recalled the soft curves of Katherine's body as he'd held her against him the night before, the sweet, womanly smell of her skin, the way she tasted on his tongue. He let the cool air of the refrigerator play against his face before slamming the door closed.

He needed a break. Period.

The phone rang, its trilling noise slicing through the silence of the room like a knife. He snatched it up instantly. "Stone."

"Hi, hon," his mother answered. "I was expecting your answering machine."

Aaron couldn't help but smile. It was his mother's standard response whenever he answered the phone himself. "No, it's me, live and in person."

"Are you working?"

Aaron considered the question before answering. "Yeah, but I haven't forgotten who the real boss is. What's up?"

"Nothing, really. I've just been concerned about Katherine since you two left the get-together so abruptly."

Aaron rubbed his forehead. He was up for just

about any conversation except the one he was about to have. "She's fine, thanks," he finally said. His gut twisted painfully as he recalled their lovemaking. "I saw her last night."

There was an audible sigh on the other end of the line. "Thank heavens," his mother replied. "I was afraid I had upset her by telling her about Jacqueline."

It took a moment for the words to sink in, then it hit him full force. His mother had told Katherine about Jacqueline. . . .

He ran his hand through his hair and resisted the urge to throw the phone across the room. What a fool he'd been to even consider that Katherine had some kind of psychic ability. Maybe she'd known about Jacqueline before the holiday, or maybe she hadn't. It didn't matter. She'd learned everything she needed to know from his own mother.

"You told her about Jacqueline?"

"I'm sorry, Aaron. She assured me that she already knew—"

A mechanical beep sounded, signaling a second call coming in. The interruption was both annoying and welcome. What else could he say to his mother without admitting that he'd brought a murder suspect to a family gathering?

"Mom? Sorry to cut you off, but I have another call. Can I give you a ring later?"

"Promise?"

"I promise," he said before pressing the switch hook to take the second call. "Stone," he answered again, hoping this call would be better than the first. It wasn't.

"Aaron, this is Dawson."

"Yes, Lieutenant."

"We've been trying to reach you." The lieutenant sounded slightly annoyed. "We've had a break in the Blake case."

Aaron wasn't sure he wanted to hear the rest. "What kind of break?" he asked.

"We're issuing a warrant for Katherine Jackson's arrest."

Aaron's mind formed a thousand questions, all of which froze in his throat.

"Some kids were playing around in the alley behind the herb shop where she works and found a small box full of some kind of white powder," the lieutenant continued. "Jacobs went and checked it out. Turns out it was half a kilo of cocaine."

"But that doesn't—"

"The packaging and the box matched the cocaine found at the scene of the Blake murder." Dawson hesitated, and Aaron could hear the soft rustle of papers being shuffled. "Listen, Aaron, I have a feeling you've gotten too close to this case. Is there something you want to tell me?"

Too close to the case . . . Aaron almost laughed at the irony of the situation. He recalled the innocent expression on Katherine's face as she sipped the wine, the uncertainty in her eyes as she emerged wearing the evening gown. But the cruelest memory of all was how their bodies fit together so perfectly, how she'd mirrored his passion. Aaron shook his head. He'd avoided facing his feelings for Katherine—had been too afraid of what he'd find.

Well, now he didn't have to. His gut twisted with betrayal. There was no longer any point.

"No." His voice sounded gruff, even to his own ears as he answered the lieutenant's question. "There's nothing else to say." He cleared his throat. "I'd like to be the one to bring her in."

"Be my guest, but make it quick."

"You got it." Aaron hung up the phone.

It would be quick but not painless. He'd had a one-two punch in the last five minutes. Dread rose up to face him. Why had he volunteered to bring Katherine in? Was he hoping for some last-minute explanation, an apology, a profession of love?

His thoughts stilled. A profession of love. He'd been betrayed, used, made a fool of—and still the one thing that came to the surface, the one thing he ached for, was for Katherine to love him.

My God, *he* was in love with *her*.

Aaron curled his right hand into a fist and slammed it into the wall. His entire body ached with betrayal, with longing for something—someone—he could no longer have.

No, it was far too late for painless.

Freedom. Jacqueline looked at the trailer park through the dusty windshield. Birds chirped in the dim morning light, and a few scattered lights glowed from inside the other trailers. Though she'd never met any of her neighbors face-to-face, she would always be grateful that one of them had cared enough to call the police—and she would always be grateful to that person for bringing Aaron into her life.

She smiled. And she would be equally as grateful to leave this trailer park behind.

At first she'd been hurt by Aaron's words, by the ultimatum he'd given her. He'd made it clear that either she should find the courage to leave, or he would no longer be there to pick up the broken pieces. He wouldn't watch her suffer any longer.

She'd been hurt and confused, but in the end she'd realized he'd issued the ultimatum out of love for her. It was what she needed to hear.

And now it was up to her to save herself.

Jacqueline depressed the clutch and eased the car into first gear, wincing as if the mechanical scraping sound would give her away. The gravel road that led from the trailer park beckoned to her. A new life. She pressed the gas, and the car moved forward, gravel popping beneath the tires.

She reached the end of the gravel drive and turned left onto the two-lane country road that marked her freedom. Her new beginning.

Her mind drifted as the minutes passed, putting precious distance between her old life and her new. She forced herself to slow as the car took a sharp curve. Day or night, Aaron had said. She could come to him day or night.

The sound of another car's engine broke her thoughts, then a flash of red in her rearview mirror caught her eye. A red car. His car. Her husband.

Fear hit her square in the stomach. No! Her fingers gripped the steering wheel as her car took a second sharp turn. It wasn't supposed to be this way. Her gaze flew back to the mirror. She couldn't see the face, but she knew with the certainty of someone doomed to fate, that it was him.

How had he known? He wasn't supposed to be home. His shift at work—

Tears blurred her vision as she gripped the steering wheel. It didn't matter. He'd found her, and he was going to kill her.

The road was too narrow, the curves coming upon her too fast for her to watch him in the mirror. Still, she felt him behind her as she drove. Faster, she had to go faster. A trickle of sweat traced her ear. She could barely get the air in and out of her lungs. All she could do was drive. Faster.

If she could only get to Aaron . . .

The impact nearly jarred her teeth from her gums as his car rammed into the rear of her tiny Volkswagen. A second flash of red appeared in the rearview mirror, but she couldn't focus on it. Another turn . . . she was going too fast . . . she needed to concentrate.

It was beside her then—the flash of red. This time as she looked, she saw his face. Pure hatred looked back at her. In that instant she saw what she'd seen a thousand times: accusations for crimes never committed. The flesh of his face was contorted, his dark beard outlining his mouth as he shouted angry, unheard words.

She no longer had to hear those words, she realized. No matter what happened, whether she lived or died, she would never have to hear them again.

A sad smile crossed her face as she hit the brakes.

There was no way to know what he'd intended, but suddenly his car was swerving in front of hers. Instead of ramming into her car, though, his met with nothing but air. Jacqueline realized then what was happening. She watched in horror as his car slammed against a massive oak tree that bordered the road. Suddenly something flew toward her, and she screamed as a spider's web of cracks broke across her windshield.

Jacqueline glanced to her right, just long enough to watch her husband's car careen off the rocky incline and plunge into the lake below. For a moment her soul screamed in denial. Not for the man he was, but for the man she'd once thought him to be.

When her eyes found the road again, she realized the hand of fate hadn't finished altering the picture. She could barely see through the cracked windshield. Sweat beaded against her forehead. Her car was over the center line stripe, and another curve loomed in front of her. The car was still moving too fast. Way too fast. She hit the brakes a second time and tried to control the inevitable skid. Her fingers curled around the steering wheel so tightly, her fingernails dug into her palms.

She thought, for a moment, that she'd made the curve. Until the car straightened. Then the telephone pole filled her broken line of vision like a final prophecy. She leaned into the steering wheel, trying with all her strength to turn the car, to cheat fate.

But it wasn't enough. There wasn't enough time.

There was an instant before the impact—an instant when she knew she was about to die. A calmness seeped into her, saturating every pore of her skin, every cell of her body. She relaxed her grip and closed her eyes.

She'd found her new beginning after all.

"No!" Katherine's eyes opened, but her body was paralyzed.

She stared at the ceiling, her gaze tracing a familiar

crack in the old plaster. She followed the crack to the corner of her bedroom and down to the window. The blinds were open, and from outside the late-afternoon sun streamed in, bringing with it the familiar haze of green from the oak tree outside her window. She could hear the birds, the occasional engine of a car.

Her apartment—she was in her apartment. Safe. Unharmed. But Jacqueline . . .

The tears began.

Aaron took the stairs slowly, each one a painful reminder of the grim task that lay ahead. In an odd way he felt lucky. At least the children had found the box of cocaine in the alley. Otherwise he'd still be caught in Katherine's web of deceit.

He paused as he reached the door. She'd most likely been in a hurry to get the drugs out of the Herb Shop in case it was searched, but the idea to stash it in the alley had backfired. At least the children's curiosity had stopped with opening the box. He felt a knot form between his neck and shoulder blades. If they'd been crazy enough to try it, things could have ended tragically.

He raised his fist and pounded on the door. "Katherine, open up. It's Aaron."

He thought he heard a faint shuffling from inside the apartment, but no one appeared. "Katherine—"

The door opened then, and Katherine stood just inside the threshold, her eyes red rimmed, her hair uncharacteristically loose and disheveled. He thought he heard a faint cry before she reached for him, wrapping her arms around his neck and burying her face against it.

He drew her against him despite himself. Something was wrong. She'd been crying. No, he reminded himself, something appeared wrong. Katherine was good with illusion. God knows he'd bought into it.

"Katherine, we have to talk." He tried to inject an air of authority to his voice, but it still came out as a whisper.

She pulled back and looked at him. Her eyes were puffy, and a tear eased from the corner of one eye and fell across her cheek. She was looking directly at him, but he had the uncanny feeling that she didn't really see him. It was as if she were in a world of her own.

She reached for his face and ran her fingers across his jawline, shaking her head. "I know you're angry with me, but I have to tell you what I know," she said, her voice hoarse and weak. "I've been so afraid, but it was a gift all along."

Her words didn't make sense. Drugs—was it possible that Katherine was on drugs? He was trying desperately to rethink everything he thought he'd understood about the woman.

He tried to pull her hands away from his face, but his fingers refused to grip her wrists. He ended up caressing the warm center of her palms instead. Hadn't he planted kisses there when they'd made love?

He shook his head, trying to cling to some shred of logic. Everything they'd shared had been a lie. But the warmth of her body, the love in her touch—whether real or imaginary—were stealing his rational thoughts.

Aaron realized, then, that they were standing, exposed, on the staircase landing. He was there to arrest her, dammit, not comfort her for whatever delusion she was having. "I don't understand, Katherine. Let me in. We have to talk."

She nodded and reached for his hand, tugging him behind her like a needy child. He endured the contact of their hands with mixed emotions—remembering the pleasure of her familiar touch, yet trying to cling to the anger that would see him through what he was about to do. He removed his hand from hers as they reached her living room, thinking the cheerfully patterned sofa and the peaceful hum of the overhead ceiling fan were a strange contrast to the bitterness that pulsed through him.

Katherine never took her eyes off him, and more than once he had to clench his fist to keep from reaching for her as she swayed.

He cleared his throat and took a step away from her. "You weren't making sense out there. What's wrong?"

She pressed her fingers to her mouth as if to keep herself from crying. "I'm trying to tell you about Jacqueline, Aaron. I dreamed about her again." She shook her head, her eyes brimming with tears. "Only this time I dreamed the last dream. I—I dreamed about her death."

The charade—the betrayal—was suddenly more than he could bear. Aaron grabbed her by the shoulders, roughly lifting her so that their eyes met. "Enough! Do you hear me, Katherine? Enough is enough!"

Her eyes were round with surprise, her lips parted

as if she couldn't form the right words. "Y-you don't believe me, I know. But why are you so angry?"

He shoved her away from him and turned to brace himself—his anger—against the solid structure of the kitchen table. His fingers gripped the edge of the thick old wood as his thoughts reeled. Should he give her a chance to bury herself even deeper, or should he just tell her outright that she was under arrest?

She touched his shoulder, and he jumped as if he'd been burned.

"I promise you on my life that I'm telling the truth."

"Save it." He turned to face her. "I'm here to arrest you."

She staggered back a few steps. "Arrest me? You can't be serious."

"The half kilo of cocaine found at the shop tends to make me very serious."

"What?" Her expression was incredulous—and very convincing. "What on earth are you talking about, Aaron?"

"I'm talking about the coke stashed in the alley next to the Herb Shop." He closed the distance between them and looked down into her face. "Did you ever consider what might happen if someone innocent stumbled on it? Good Lord, Katherine, two little boys found the box. If they'd tried it, they could likely have ended up dead."

"Cocaine." The word wasn't a question, but a flat statement instead, as if she were mulling over the possibility that such a thing existed. "That's impossible." Her eyes were narrow, suspicious now. "You found cocaine . . . in a box . . . near the Herb Shop?" She shook her head. "Cheryl signs for all our deliveries, and the only boxes we leave outdoors go directly into the trash. Aaron, if you found cocaine at the Herb Shop, then you've either made a mistake or someone is trying to set me up."

He leaned toward her, wanting to unnerve her, needing to draw a reaction from her. Instead, he found himself trying to ignore the rush of regret he felt. He thought they'd had something special, some connection. . . .

"Not only did we find the drugs, but the cocaine matched that at the scene of the crime."

"The scene of the crime?"

"Oh, of course. You've probably forgotten. My mistake." He threw his hands in the air. "I was referring to the cocaine found next to Owen Blake's body. The wrapping was identical to the bundles found in the alley—with the exception of the blood, of course."

She staggered back from him, her hand cradling the base of her throat, her fair complexion paling to a blue-white. He thought she was going to be sick, until a blush of color reddened her cheeks. The color grew until she was completely flushed and her eyes sparked with determination.

"No." She shook her head and started toward him, her hands fumbling to grip his arms. When she clutched at him, he felt her fingers dig painfully into his flesh before she spoke again. "Listen to me, Aaron. I don't know why—I don't even know how—all of this is happening to us. But I'm telling you the truth—"

"Oh, so I guess Jacqueline was just an added

touch?" He tried to remove her hands from his arms, but she wouldn't budge. "Well, I must admit it threw my judgment off nicely."

"No!" The word was almost a scream. "I didn't lie about Jacqueline. That's what I've been trying to tell you."

The wild look in Katherine's eyes bordered on manic, and Aaron felt a disturbing fear gnaw at the pit of his stomach. Was she crazy? Oh God, somewhere along the way he'd accepted the fact that she was guilty, but . . . An image of Katherine being institutionalized flashed in his head. He wasn't prepared to face that.

She took advantage of his silence. "Aaron, listen to me. I closed the shop early today to get some rest. I fell asleep when I came home, and I dreamed about Jacqueline again, only this time—"

"I don't want to hear it, Katherine!"

"—she didn't kill herself, *he* killed her."

The first of her words were lost to him, but the last registered loud and clear.

. . . *he killed her.*

"What?"

He shouldn't have even dignified her desperate rambling with a response, but the single word was out before he'd had time to think. God, but she was good at striking a nerve. And judging from the hopeful look in her eyes, she knew she'd found an opening.

"Her husband killed her." Tears formed at the corners of her eyes. "He ran her off the road." She blinked once, a tired expression replacing the near-hysteria of a few moments ago. "She hit a telephone pole, didn't she?"

Aaron felt an old anger tighten in his chest. Maybe she was crazy, or maybe she was just a liar. In either case, he was finished with her. He allowed himself one last appreciative glance at her. She was seductive beauty and innocence all wrapped up in one. He jerked free of her grasp to turn his back to her.

He was nobody's fool. At least not twice.

"Yeah." His voice faltered, and he mentally cursed the weakness. He cleared his throat and allowed the distaste he felt for Katherine register in his tone. "She hit a telephone pole and died instantly. Just like the newspapers reported."

"You told her to choose." Katherine's voice was barely a whisper, but it whipped his head around as if she'd slapped him. "And she was coming to you."

He shook his head in denial. "What do you mean?"

His mind spun with possibilities in the breath of silence that followed. It wasn't possible. He'd lived with that secret alone, borne the weight of guilt for an action that he was solely responsible for. No, she couldn't know that he'd forced Jacqueline to choose between her old life and a new one . . . with him.

"You told her to choose—you gave her an ultimatum." Katherine's smile was weak, but her eyes held a certain peace. "Believe what I'm telling you, Aaron. She was coming to you."

NINE

Katherine watched Aaron's face alter and knew he believed her. Or at least he wanted to, and that was a start.

This time when she stepped toward him, he didn't turn away. She cupped his face with her hands, her heart swelling with love for him, her body warming at the feel of his rough jaw beneath her fingertips.

She loved this man.

Maybe it was because she'd come so near to losing him, or perhaps it was closing the final chapter on Jacqueline's life, but she knew with certainty that she loved Aaron in a way that could never be duplicated with another man. He was the other half of her soul, the only man she would ever love completely.

She had to make him believe her.

"She knew you loved her." Katherine met his eyes, saw the disbelief mixed with longing. "She knew you only asked her to choose because you couldn't bear to see her hurt."

"What are you trying to prove—" He shook his head and started to pull back.

Katherine urged his face back toward hers, her eyes never leaving his. "I can give you all the proof you need if you'll let me."

"How?" His voice was a hoarse whisper, his expression a myriad of tangled emotions.

"Because he's there—Jacqueline's husband. He's there in the lake that borders the road. He made her lose control of her car. Then his own car went off the road and into the water."

"That's not possible." Aaron's eyes narrowed in suspicion. "We searched for anything that could have caused the accident. There was nothing. No skid marks—nothing."

Katherine closed her eyes and summoned the image from her dream. Where had Jacqueline been when she'd first seen the flash of red? "She was on a hill," Katherine said, her eyes still closed in concentration. "There was a sharp curve. Then she saw him—he was following her."

"You know this . . . from the dream?" There was no sarcasm in Aaron's voice this time.

"Yes." Katherine nodded. "She was going down a hill. The curves were sharp. He came up beside her, and Jacqueline hit the brakes." She opened her eyes and met Aaron's gaze. "She didn't know he was about to try to run her off the road. Instead of ramming her car, the momentum caused him to hit a tree, then go off the incline and into the water."

"My God . . ." Aaron took a small step toward her. "We never investigated that far up the incline."

She stared at him and thought her heart would burst with happiness. His blue eyes were stormy with emotion, but the disdain she'd seen there earlier was gone. Was it possible that he believed her? She had to be certain.

"Take me there, Aaron. I'll find the tree he hit. Surely it would still have the scar. Take me there and I'll prove it to you. His car has to still be submerged. But we can—"

"Then why? Why did she lose control?" Aaron frowned, his eyes boring into hers without seeing.

He was with Jacqueline, she realized. Her heart froze in her chest. Of course. He still loved her.

Katherine began to tremble with fatigue—fatigue that had been held at bay by the hope that she and Aaron still had a chance. "Something hit the windshield. I don't know. She couldn't see—the window was shattered. Then there were the curves. They were too sharp, and she was going too fast." Katherine shook her head. "She just couldn't get control of the car. Then there was the telephone pole—"

A sob escaped her, and she clamped her hand over her mouth. Aaron pulled her into his arms, cradling her head against the crook of his neck. She needed him so badly that she ached. Being held in his arms at this moment was the most bittersweet feeling of all. She relished his warmth, his strength, his touch.

But it couldn't last. His heart still belonged to Jacqueline.

"Are you okay?" His voice was deep and low, his own emotions vibrating just below the surface.

She nodded against his shoulder. "She was coming

to you. You have to believe that. After all this time you deserve to know the truth."

"Katherine, I swear, if you're lying—"

"I'm not."

He pulled back and pressed the palm of his hand against her damp cheek. "Then I don't deserve you."

His lips found hers before she could answer, and her own response to his kiss flowed from her, answering him without the need for words. She pressed her body against the long, hard mass of his, relishing his strength, drawing courage from his very presence.

He slid his mouth from hers. "Thank you for giving me the truth," he whispered against her cheek. "My God, if only things could have ended differently."

"I'm so sorry." She tried to pull away. "I know you're still in love with her."

His grip tightened. "No—"

"With her memory, I mean. Believe me, I understand—"

Aaron laughed, but the laughter was born of pain. "No, Katherine. I've been tortured by the memory of her. I was so young, wanted so desperately to help that I thought I was in love. Then somewhere along the line, after Jacqueline's death, I decided that love wasn't for me." He smoothed a tendril of hair from her eyes. "It just hurt too damned much. But you changed all that. The minute I fell in love with you, I knew I wanted a second chance."

"What?" The question was out before his words thoroughly registered in her mind.

He was in love with her? Every possibility she'd denied herself over the years took root and grew—

grew into a beautiful dream that held the promise of a real future. One with Aaron.

"Surely you know I'm in love with you." He smiled down at her. "You know everything else."

Katherine's mind raced to find a way to tell him how much she loved him, but couldn't. She hadn't uttered those words since she was eight years old; she wasn't even sure she was capable of saying them anymore. Instead, as she reached for him, she let her body speak for her. Her hardened nipples met his chest as their bodies touched, and she pressed her mouth against the base of his neck.

Only she was aware of the subtle changes as her body readied itself for him. And she would have him. A purely female response coiled deep in the core of her body. She leaned her head against his shoulder and waited for his response. Their bodies were made for each other as surely as the mental link that bound them together—that had brought them together in the first place.

"What you have is a gift," he whispered, his mouth moving against her hair. "Do you realize that?"

"Now I do." She shook her head. "It's frightened me for years. I didn't know how to recognize it, how to just relax and let it happen."

He pulled her tighter against him, his hands tangling in her hair and pressing her face against his chest. "What about us? Are you willing to let us happen?"

She recognized the husky tone to his voice, and felt his heart accelerate beneath her cheek. She lifted her head and met his eyes. "There's nothing I want more."

He brought her hips to his, his arousal nudging

against her through the thin cotton slacks she wore. She parted her legs slightly, allowing him more intimate contact.

She'd always felt her body was too big, too blatantly curvy and feminine. But not with Aaron. The firm, masculine planes of his chest contrasted perfectly with the fullness of her breasts, and his narrow, muscular hips fit exactly between her soft thighs. She slid her hands around his hips, urging him to move against her. Pleasure radiated from the contact, and she knew from experience that his body would fill every inch of her completely.

"I want you, Katherine," he breathed against her ear as his hips urged her legs farther apart. "Now."

She entwined her fingers in his and tugged him down onto the sofa. As they sank together into the soft cushions, Aaron's hands were already tugging at the buttons of her blouse, seeking—and finding—her breasts beneath her bra. In the breath of a moment, the front closure of the bra was loosened, and his mouth was against her flesh. Hot and moist, his tongue encircled one areola, then moved away in maddening denial to trace the fullness of her to the base of her rib cage.

"You're so beautiful."

He stole any words of response as his lips found hers. The slant of his mouth fit perfectly over hers as his thumbs hooked over the elastic waistband of her cotton slacks, forcing them past her hips.

Skin to skin. The contact actually startled her. When had he removed his jeans? It must have been before—when his mouth was on her—

He entered her then, in one swift motion that left

her gasping for breath and her heart pounding with the ecstasy of the sudden fullness. Just as her body accepted him, he began moving. Hot flesh against hot flesh. There was no ceremony this time, no holding back—just the raw mating of man and woman pleasing each other with their bodies, secure in knowing their love was returned.

The rhythm of his hips was one glorious motion, withdrawing and entering without pause. Her body warmed, drawing him farther inside her as he thrust. The feeling, the pleasure, was so perfect that she wanted to prolong their togetherness. Her fingers found the muscled flesh of his hips, intending to slow him, but the thought wouldn't fully form. Not with Aaron's body moving inside hers, not with the promise of release rising within her.

A low moan escaped him, and he lowered his mouth to her breasts. He sucked one nipple into his mouth, sending shock waves of pleasure through Katherine's body. He placed his hands on either side of her breasts, drawing the flesh of them up to receive lavish treatment from his mouth. He moved from one to the other, stopping only long enough to bring her nearly to the edge of release.

Only then did she realize the movement of his hips had paused, and her own hips lifted in frantic need. "Aaron, I can't wait—"

"Then don't," he whispered. With a low moan he buried himself deep within her.

Together they found release, the hot, sticky moistness of Aaron's seed spilling into her and soaking the discarded clothing that lay beneath them.

They lay curled against each other for what seemed like forever, yet like mere seconds at the same time. "Weren't you supposed to arrest someone?" she finally whispered against his ear.

Aaron rolled to his side, easing himself from her body but never releasing his hold on her. "Don't remind me," he said, nuzzling his rough jaw against her neck.

"Seriously, Aaron, what are you going to do? How are you going to explain about me?" The reality of the situation crept back, and she felt a twinge of panic. "Someone must have planted the drugs—"

"Whoa. Slow down."

"Sorry." She rested her head against his shoulder and tried to relax. "I just don't get it. Who would want to set me up?"

He groaned. "You really don't believe in basking in the afterglow, do you?"

Katherine couldn't help but smile, knowing she'd gone from one extreme to the other. Still, if she and Aaron were going to have a chance at a future together, she was going to have to get to the bottom of what was going on. "The most important thing in the world to me right now is that you believe me."

"I believe you." He responded without hesitation. His fingers traced the line of her jaw before drawing a handful of silky hair to his face. She smelled like wildflowers and felt like heaven against him.

She'd unintentionally taught him how to love again, and he, just as unintentionally, had learned the lesson. Aaron felt his body begin to stir with arousal. Unbelievable, he thought, and forced himself to sit upright. Away from temptation.

"What will you tell them?" she asked. "What will you say when you don't bring me in?"

She was right, of course. He was going to have to tell the lieutenant something. "You weren't home," he answered a bit gruffly.

"But then what? They'll eventually—"

He leaned down and planted a thorough kiss on her lips. "I don't know," he said. "But right now I'll start with what we've got." He met her eyes. "I'm going to the scene of Jacqueline's accident. I have answers, but now I need to come up with some proof. It may seem flimsy, but we need to prove that you really do have abilities. It would, at least to some degree, explain why you called the inn." He shrugged. "It's all we have."

She nodded. "It's just that I've barely come to terms with—with knowing things. I can hardly imagine someone else believing it."

Her eyes were round with fear, their almost luminescent green color shining with purity. She trusted him. He wanted to tell her he could solve their problems, find the answers and the proof that would show everyone else what they already knew to be true. But he couldn't promise her that.

"Come with me," he said.

"No." She smiled and shook her head. "I think that's something you need to do by yourself. I said good-bye to Jacqueline when the last dream ended. You need a chance to do the same."

Aaron couldn't argue with her logic. He'd spent the last ten years of his life wishing he could ease the guilt and the pain. Katherine had given him that gift. But he still needed to say good-bye to Jacqueline.

And prove Katherine's innocence to the rest of the world.

"Wait here." He stepped into his underwear and tugged on his jeans before heading toward the bathroom. As he pulled Katherine's robe from a peg behind the door, the sound of a car's engine caught his attention. He leaned against the windowsill and looked out the small bathroom window to the street below. A patrol car cruised slowly down the street.

Damn! Someone other than the lieutenant knew he was there. No, he reminded himself, he'd parked out of view in the alley a block over. He hadn't known at the time why he'd chosen to park his car in the alley, but now it was clear to him. He had wanted Katherine to prove him wrong, and he hadn't wanted any interference.

Aaron smiled. And she had proved him wrong. He had no doubt that he'd find Jacqueline's husband's car in the lake. Any and all doubt had vanished when she'd told him about the ultimatum. He'd lived with that secret for the last ten years. In his mind he'd wondered—feared—that Jacqueline had killed her husband before killing herself. After all, he'd seemed to vanish off the face of the earth the day of her accident. And in his worst nightmares, Aaron had accepted the blame for that too. But now he had the truth. Thanks to Katherine.

The patrol car, however, proved that someone knew he was supposed to be here. Which meant he needed to get busy. They might never find Owen

Blake's killer. Unfortunately drug-related murders often ended that way. But he would clear Katherine of suspicion. He had to.

He returned to the living room and held the robe out for her. As she stood and stepped into the soft material, he caught her against him in a hug. "Keep a low profile for the rest of the day. Okay?"

"Okay." She checked her watch. "I have a few things to do, but I'll stay out of sight."

He turned her by the shoulders and lowered his mouth to hers, loving the feel of her lips against his, the very taste of her. "I'll call you as soon as I get back."

She nodded. "Thank you."

"For what?"

"For believing me."

He glanced back as he reached the door. "I should have done that earlier."

Aaron scanned the street for any sign of the patrol car as he closed the door behind him. Nothing. He made his way down the outside stairs and across the lawn that separated the duplex from the alley. Maybe it had been a routine patrol after all, nothing connected to Katherine or the arrest he was supposed to have made.

Then why did he feel such urgency? He forced himself to walk as he entered the alley. He'd gone no more than twenty yards when something metallic caught his eye. Aaron slowed his pace and headed toward the source that reflected the late-afternoon sun. Lying in a patch of overgrown grass at the edge of the alley was a flashlight. He knelt down next to it and parted the weeds. Next to the flashlight was a screwdriver.

A neighbor making repairs? He glanced around at the older homes that were adjacent to Katherine's duplex. Neatly trimmed lawns and ancient oak trees were all that bordered the alley. There weren't many children in the neighborhood, no fences being reparied, no wayward dogs. Aaron looked up and found he had a perfect view of Katherine's house—and Katherine's bedroom—from where he was.

A familiar tightening in his gut told him something wasn't right. The image of Roscoe bound with duct tape flashed in his head. He had believed Katherine when she'd said an intruder had entered the house, but logic hadn't allowed him to entirely dismiss the idea that she'd staged the whole thing.

Until today.

A sick feeling crept over him. Now it was painfully obvious that they hadn't done everything they should have to find out what had happened. More specifically, to find out who would have wanted to harm Katherine—and why.

Aaron hurried on to his car and lifted the radio microphone as he got in. He held it in his hand without depressing the talk button, his mind spinning with unanswered questions. Finally he replaced it. He couldn't radio for someone to come and take a look around without possibly alerting them to the fact that Katherine was home.

He wouldn't be gone long, he reasoned. And Katherine had agreed to stay put, it was broad daylight, and an officer was already in the area. Satisfied, Aaron cranked the car.

His hand still rested on the gearshift when he saw her. She stood on the outside stoop of the duplex, one hand against the doorknob as she glanced around. She had changed clothes, he noticed. Her hair, pulled into a ponytail, cascaded out beneath a light blue baseball cap, and her robe had been replaced by blue jeans and a white tank top.

"Dammit, Katherine, get back in the house—" His words were cut short as he watched her turn and lock the door behind her, then slide on a pair of sunglasses. Apparently she had no intention of going back inside.

Before he could open the car door, she bounded down the stairs and crossed the lawn to her own car. Aaron slammed the gearshift into drive. Leaving Katherine safely locked in her apartment was one thing, but he wasn't about to leave her traipsing around town, vulnerable and alone.

She was already a block ahead of him when he pulled out of the alley. Wherever she was going, she was determined to get there fast. He cursed as he came to a four-way stop, and Katherine continued almost out of sight. He flashed his headlights, but her car never slowed. He considered turning on his emergency lights, but hesitated. The last thing he wanted to do was to call attention to them.

When he finally caught sight of her car again, he decided his luck had changed. She waited just ahead at a notoriously slow stoplight. But before he could reach her, a patrol car pulled out of a side street and slipped in behind her. Aaron slowed, knowing he would be easily spotted in his department-issued car.

He popped a piece of gum in his mouth and forced himself to take a side street to avoid being seen. He wasn't certain, but the driver in the patrol car looked like Jacobs, and he knew that the rookie, who had been all over him like a bad puppy lately, would spot him in a second.

The side street ran parallel to the one Katherine was on, and Aaron matched her speed, tracking her at every stop sign, every red light. Finally, as she pulled out of the residential area and onto a busy highway, the patrol car headed in the opposite direction. Aaron breathed a sigh of relief as he maneuvered through the last of the stop signs and pulled onto the highway behind Katherine.

Dammit, she hadn't given the slightest indication that she was going to leave the apartment. If she had, he would have put a stop to the idea before ever leaving. What exactly had she said? That she had a few things to do, he recalled. Well, leaving the apartment was a bad idea, even before he found the flashlight and screwdriver in the alley. Now, if he possessed a single instinct in his body, he knew it was more than that. It was dangerous.

Where was she going? The farther away from the city they traveled, the less at ease he felt. Aaron was even more puzzled as Katherine took a seldom used exit that led to a rural area. Sandwiched between busy suburban regions, this pocket of land remained undeveloped because of its steep and rugged terrain. Easy to get to but isolated, it was also well known in law enforcement circles as a high-crime area. So why on earth was Katherine going there?

Aaron stayed back out of sight, an odd curiosity now taking priority. A feeling of dread hit him as she made a hasty turn onto a single-lane dirt road that led up the side of one mountain, then skidded to a stop in front of a heavy, padlocked chain. His mind scrambled to make sense of the situation, to come up with some plausible reason for her to be headed into the middle of nowhere when she was supposed to be at home—safe and waiting for him.

He bypassed the dirt road, then circled back and turned onto it, his tires bumping over the chain that now lay, unlocked, across the road. He crept up the mountainside, the trail Katherine took still easily traced by the billowing cloud of dust her car had left in its wake. After trailing her for a minute, Aaron pulled off the dirt road and into a side pocket that had, no doubt, seen its share of teenage lovers. But today it served as the perfect shield, its overgrown vines and thick shrubs hiding his car.

Why did he feel the need to hide from Katherine? Why not just catch up to her and give her a piece of his mind for leaving the apartment? Because it didn't make sense, that's why. She'd changed clothes and shot out of the apartment like an arrow, broken every speed limit in town, and had headed into an area that a seasoned police officer would think twice about before entering alone.

Aaron stepped out of the car, leaving the door ajar. He crossed the tangle of vines and underbrush that hid his vehicle and made his way to the side of the road.

Silently he walked up the dirt clearing until he was almost to the top of the steep incline. As he rounded a sharp curve, he shielded his eyes from the late-afternoon sun and gazed up the mountainside. Katherine's car was parked in full view at the end of the road.

"What the hell—" He forced himself to remain still as he caught sight of Katherine scrambling up the side of the treacherous mountain on her hands and knees.

Whatever she was doing, and wherever she thought she was going, she was sure of herself. Aaron inched up the road a few yards farther, never taking his eyes off her. She had stopped on the side of the incline and was kneeling down. He frowned as he watched her reach into the back pocket of her jeans, pull out a pencil and piece of paper, and write something on it.

Then he saw it—a small red tag encircling a plant next to her. He felt his pulse accelerate with dread as she reached down and gingerly fingered the leaves. He was still at least thirty yards away from her, but even from his less-than-perfect vantage point, he could make out the five slender leaves of the young marijuana plant.

In that moment her innocence shattered. Every doubt he'd had about Katherine came flying back at him, hitting him square in the chest—and in the heart.

She looked up then, as if sensing someone watching her. Aaron froze in his spot by the roadside, and eventually Katherine turned her attention back to the plant, his presence apparently unnoticed. He squinted against the glare of the sun as it glimmered over the top of the mountain, watching Katherine as she returned the piece of paper to her pocket and moved on to a second plant.

"Dammit . . ." he heard himself whisper, and took a step back in disbelief. He looked at the wooded area that surrounded Katherine. Now that he knew what to look for, he was amazed he hadn't noticed right away. At least two dozen red tags marked plants growing on the mountainside.

He considered walking up casually behind her, asking her to explain what she could, finally, not explain away. Heaven knew he'd been eager enough to accept her crazy answers in the past. Crazy. He stifled a laugh. He might not be crazy, but gullible definitely applied. He'd lapped up anything and everything she'd fed him like a hungry pup.

But what about Jacqueline? How could she have known that he thought he was responsible for her death? A lucky guess? You gullible fool, his mind taunted. The guilt had been written all over his face, and Katherine had been just smart enough to read it.

Aaron felt his fingers curl around the door handle of his car, and was surprised to find that he'd returned to it. He hadn't realized he'd made the decision to leave, but now that he was standing next to the car, he knew—right or wrong—that he had to get away.

Fast.

He would never be able to justify not confronting her, but she didn't appear to be going anywhere. That fact caused a swell of anger to rise in him. She'd been confident enough to come here in broad daylight, and arrogant enough to take her time with the plants.

His mind flashed to the gentle stroke of her fingertips against the leaves, but his body recalled another soft touch. The touch of her fingers against his back, the gentle pressure of her fingernails as he'd pressed himself into her welcoming flesh, making their bodies one.

Aaron sank down into the driver's seat. He could feel his pulse pounding in his temples, and absently placed his hands against his head. It had been years since he'd felt this kind of anguish.

Ten years, to be exact.

He had been so sure about Katherine, so sure she wasn't capable of murder, wasn't capable of being involved with drugs. For a moment he considered the possibility that she could still be innocent of those charges. Suppose growing the plants was some misguided attempt to use them for their medicinal value, suppose she was still innocent of the other charges—

Fool, the voice of reason interrupted. *Trust what you've seen with your own eyes.*

Aaron suddenly felt twice his age. Tired. He was so damned tired.

He turned the key in the ignition and slammed the car into reverse, sending a spray of last year's leaves and broken underbrush behind him. For once in his life he wasn't ready to accept logic, wasn't willing to do the right thing.

Let someone else do it.

He felt the weight of responsibility bearing down on his shoulders like the weight of the world as he spun the car around and headed back down the mountain.

He would decide what to do about Katherine later. Right now all he wanted to do was get away—away from his mistakes, from responsibility, from temptation.

Away from Katherine.

TEN

Katherine glanced at the dirt road that led up the mountain, certain that she'd heard a car engine. Her hands stilled against the leaves of the plant as she cocked her head to listen. Nothing. Relieved, she turned her attention back to recording the plant's growth. She loved the wild beauty of the rugged mountain, always felt refreshed and centered after spending time outdoors. But as luck would have it, the best spot for growing American ginseng wasn't necessarily the safest place to be alone.

Today she'd decided the time spent outdoors would be worth whatever risk was involved. She needed the mountainside to work its magic more than ever. Aaron had said he loved her. So why couldn't she say the simple words back to him? She didn't need to ask herself if she loved him. There was no doubt about that. It had just been so long since she'd actually uttered the words.

She shook her head. It had been easy to let her

body say what she hadn't been able to vocalize. Perhaps too easy. It was ridiculous, how frightened she was to tell Aaron how she felt. She pressed the sharp edge of her trowel into the loamy earth, lifted the root from its resting place, and placed it in a small Ziploc bag. Grams would be pleased at the rate of growth. Katherine had to admit that her foster mother's determination to see the rare wild plant safely cultivated had proven contagious over the years.

Just then her foot slid against the damp leaves that covered the mountainside. Katherine watched as a miniature rock slide tumbled down the steep incline and into the valley below. It was a good thing Grams allowed her to tend the plants. It probably wouldn't be safe for the older woman to try to climb the mountain. Katherine grinned. Even so, she wasn't about to tell Grams that. She'd seen Grams's temper come alive like a sleeping giant when told she was too old to tackle something. No thank you. Katherine would let someone else tell her if the occasion ever arose.

She moved on to a second ginseng plant, measured, recorded, then harvested the delicate root. Her stomach rumbled with hunger, and she glanced at her watch. Six o'clock. So where was Aaron right now? Mixed emotions filled her as she envisioned him at the site of Jacqueline's accident. She hadn't doubted, even for a second, that he would find the proof he needed.

The proof they both needed.

What if you're wrong? the voice of doubt whispered. What if, though her other visions had been right, this one fact was a figment of her imagination, or worse, a projection of the illness she'd feared all her life? A shadow passed overhead, and the leaves of the trees swayed with an unexpected breeze. She jumped, startled, as a crow called out from the valley below.

Katherine tucked the plastic bag in the front pocket of her jeans, scooped up the trowel, and started back down the incline. There was plenty of daylight left. In fact, the mountain would probably be bathed in the golden light for another hour before dusk arrived. Still, she suddenly felt the need to go home. She swallowed down a feeling of panic as she momentarily lost her footing in the heavy underbrush. What was wrong with her? She couldn't explain it, but she had the urge to run—a gripping, illogical sense of danger.

She paused, her hand holding a gnarled dogwood sapling for balance, and forced herself to breathe, to slow down. It was simply that she needed to get home, she told herself, needed to be where Aaron could reach her when he returned. That was all. She continued down the incline again, more slowly this time, until she finally reached the level dirt road that divided the twin peaks of the mountaintop.

She pulled the Ziploc bag that held the small ginseng roots from the left front pocket of her jeans, then retrieved her car keys from the other. She felt a strange sense of relief as she finally reached her car, tossed the plastic bag into the passenger's seat, and sank down into the familiar upholstery.

She smelled the pungent scent of new leather in the instant before the gloved hand closed over her mouth. There was a flash of familiarity, then confusion as his hand jerked her head back painfully against the headrest. She wanted to scream, but terror rose up to meet her, stealing her strength.

A cracking noise—along with a sharp stab of pain—pierced her head. Light. White, blinding light flashed before her closed eyes. Then darkness. A horrible darkness that swallowed her up and pulled her down.

Down into its chasm of terrifying silence.

Aaron felt the crunch of roadside gravel beneath his feet, the muggy, warm breeze against his face as it rose from the lake and up the cliff to the road. He clenched his jaw against the pain. For ten years he'd managed to avoid this stretch of road, hadn't wanted to deal with the memories.

So why now? Why, when all he'd wanted to do was escape, had he ended up here? He glanced at the telephone pole a few yards to his left. Newer than the others that dotted the roadside, it haunted him with memories of Jacqueline's accident.

The other officers hadn't known, of course, of his friendship with Jacqueline—hadn't known to warn him. The image of her broken body, the anguish he'd seen on the faces of the other officers, the rescue workers who hadn't been able to work their magic that day, would be forever etched into his memory. He looked at the winding country road that curled dangerously close to the mountain's edge, seeming at spots to literally hover over the lake.

He knew why he was there. He hadn't intentionally driven there, hadn't thought of anything but Katherine—of the betrayal he felt—for miles. But as his car had pulled onto this winding stretch of road he'd realized he had to come back. It was time to say good-bye to Jacqueline after all, to chase the ghosts from his mind.

And, he knew, to give Katherine one last chance.

Aaron walked back to his car like a tired old man. He felt as if he'd just run a marathon and lost. God, he dreaded what he was about to do. His logical mind told him he'd find nothing, no shred of evidence to prove that Jacqueline's husband had caused her accident and had plunged from this road to his death in the lake below. No proof that Katherine had been telling the truth.

But then again, maybe he would.

He slid into the car, slammed the door behind him, and turned the key in the ignition. Something had happened to him. A sad smile crossed his face as he pulled onto the road and headed up the incline. Katherine had happened to him, and he wasn't ready to give up on her yet. As he drove he kept a sharp eye on the road. In Katherine's vision she'd seen a flash of red—Jacqueline's husband's car—come up behind her. But where? A hill, a sharp curve, she'd said. He felt his pulse accelerate as he rounded a curve and stared at a steep stretch of road that ran close to the edge of the cliff.

Aaron pulled onto a wide area on the shoulder and stepped out of his car. As he studied the road, the few trees that bordered it, and the steep, rocky cliff that tumbled toward the lake below, he knew. He couldn't explain how he knew. He no longer had to.

He walked, as if in a dream, toward a massive oak, the largest of the few trees that separated the road from the cliff. It looked as if it clung to the mountain out of sheer determination, its massive root system visible above the dirt and rocks that gave way to the cliff below. A few gnarled branches reached out over the lake below, but most leaned inward toward the road, as if cleaving to the security of the mountain. Its leaves were light green and healthy, its bark unmarred.

But Aaron knew the other side would be different.

He felt his pulse beat against his temples. With every step he took, he was more certain that the other side would be scarred with the evidence he needed. He reached out and touched the silver bark, allowing a few scaly pieces to break away beneath his hand. He circled the tree until he stood on the other side—facing the deep scar he had known would spoil the beauty of the tree.

But to him it was the most beautiful thing he'd ever seen.

The gash had been deep, and the scar that covered it bubbled over the wound like a tribute to all it had endured and survived. He turned and faced the road, and the scene of Jacqueline's accident played out before his eyes. It was so clear to him now, he marveled that it hadn't occurred to him before. He shook his head. If only it had occurred to him ten years ago.

He was drawn toward the far side of the road like a magnet. Not knowing why, but knowing he had to, he followed his instinct. His days of questioning intuition and instinct were over, he decided, as he walked headlong into the tangle of underbrush. At first nothing seemed out of place. There was a collection of leaves washed by the natural flow of rain down the mountainside and a few battered aluminum cans. Then he saw it.

Vines curled in and out of the old hubcap, and roadside dirt and debris all but covered it. Aaron reached down and tugged it from the grasp of the roots and honeysuckle vines that had adhered it to the ground. He turned it over in his hands. It could have fallen from any passing car, could belong to anyone. But it didn't. It belonged to Jacqueline's husband's car, and it had shattered her windshield. He knew it without a doubt.

Aaron walked back to the edge of the cliff and peered down at the lake. Raw anger surged through him as he stared at the glassy surface of the water. In the water below him was the body of a man who had caused two deaths ten years ago—besides his own. Jacqueline had died that day, but so had a part of Aaron. His shoulders slumped with an old, familiar guilt. He'd wanted desperately to help, but in the end he'd failed. If only he'd been mature enough to know that Jacqueline needed more from him than good advice. And ultimatums.

He walked back to the tree and pressed his forehead against the trunk. Slowly he ran his hand over the scar, feeling the strength of the new wood that covered the old wound. He wanted to cry unshed tears, wanted revenge against a dead man, wanted to scream.

Instead, he wordlessly said good-bye to Jacqueline and thanked her for finding a way to reach back to him, to bring Katherine into his life. The part of him that had died ten years before was the part that mattered most—his ability to love. But Katherine had given that back to him.

Aaron lifted his head, feeling as if his vision had cleared for the first time in a decade. He headed back to the car and pulled the mike from the radio unit. "Fifty-one to dispatch."

He massaged his temples in the pause that followed. He couldn't explain what Katherine had been doing on the hillside that afternoon, but he had a sudden, overwhelming feeling that he'd been wrong—dead wrong.

"Dispatch to fifty-one. Go ahead."

"I need Johnny Jacobs dispatched to the utility access area off of Millstown Road, to follow up on a Katherine Jackson in the area."

"Copy."

"He should already be in the area. Tell him to monitor the situation but make no arrest until I can get there."

Aaron turned the hubcap over in his hands as he waited on a confirmation. There would be an explanation for what Katherine was doing on the mountainside. He was certain of it. As certain as he was that the car lay hidden beneath the lake. He tossed the hubcap into the passenger's seat and raked his soiled fingers against his jeans. His mind drifted over other accusations—Owen Blake, the telephone call, the cocaine found in the alley . . .

"Fifty-one, that's a negative on Jacobs. He went inactive at fifteen hundred hours. Should I dispatch another officer?"

Aaron held the mike loosely in his grip. Jacobs had

gone inactive at three o'clock that afternoon? He'd obviously driven by Katherine's house more than once since then—

"Fifty-one, do you copy?"

"Uh—yes. Negative on a second dispatch."

Aaron felt the fine hairs on the back of his neck rise. *Negative on Jacobs* . . . Those words were hauntingly familiar. He'd heard them the night Katherine's apartment had been broken into.

His mind raced ahead, consuming facts like a wildfire out of control. *Negative on Jacobs. He's not responding.* . . . The words jumped out of his memory. Aaron shook his head. Jacobs had supposedly been working Roadie's Bar the night Katherine's apartment had been broken into. He should have been available, he should have answered the dispatch.

He *shouldn't* have been circling Katherine's apartment that afternoon if he was off duty. Aaron's stomach clenched as if someone had punched him. It was Jacobs who'd processed the cocaine found in the alley, who was so eager to see the Blake case closed. *But next time tell that rookie not to screw with the air conditioner or anything else.* . . . A rush of nausea hit him full force as he recalled Mickey's words.

Dear God, he'd missed the obvious. Aaron cranked the engine, then spun the car in a circle and pointed it toward the city.

"I promise you on my life that I'm telling the truth." Katherine's words echoed in his head.

"Please," he prayed through clenched teeth, "don't let me fail this time."

She couldn't breathe.

"Wake up, dammit, and answer me!"

Acrid fumes stung her eyes and nostrils. Finally her breath rushed violently from her lungs, and Katherine sucked in cool, damp air. Think. She couldn't think. She shivered, though she could tell the room was warm. Something was wrong. Her hands were tied—

Someone grasped her shoulders from behind, digging his fingers into the sensitive flesh between her collarbone and neck.

"I said who the hell are you?"

The man was angry—he frightened her. Where was she? Indoors. No, wait. She could hear crickets. And there was hardly any light. Musty. The room smelled musty. "What—?" She tried to speak, but could only choke on her own words.

Something was stinging her throat, making her eyes tear. Ammonia—that's what it was. He had waved the fumes beneath her nose. Katherine froze with fear. She had been to the mountain . . . had returned to her car . . .

He shook her shoulders. One—two—three times. In her mind she ticked off the number of shakes like a schoolgirl practicing simple arithmetic, but the pain was all too real. It shot down her spinal column and up the base of her neck.

"Stop." She heard her own voice as if from a distance.

The man moved around and squatted down before her. Disbelief filled her as her gaze settled on the badge that reflected the room's dim lighting. A cop? Momentary hope rose, then died just as quickly. She recognized his face—he had been with Aaron the day she drove to the inn.

"Oh, I see we've found our voice. Good." He rose and stretched his thin frame as if he were bored. "That's real good."

Katherine blinked against the image of . . . She couldn't remember his name. Was it Jacob? She tried to concentrate, but couldn't get beyond the raw anger, the danger in his eyes. He was supposedly a policeman. She was certain of that much. But why would a police officer be treating her like this? What had she done?

He pulled his gun from his holster, cocked it, and placed it against her right temple. Katherine's body went cold, yet beads of sweat trickled between her breasts, dampened the loose armholes of her tank top.

"Start at the beginning." His voice was low and smooth, unlike earlier. "How are you connected with Owen Blake?"

"I—I'm not." She despised the tremor she heard in her voice. "I didn't even know him."

His fingers dug into the soft flesh of her upper arm, and he jerked her upward against the barrel of the gun. "Try again, sweetheart. I was there when your call came in."

Terror gripped her. Her first inclination was to blurt out the truth, try to explain the telephone call. But how could she expect him to believe her? She choked on a hysterical laugh. No, he would probably pull the trigger to teach her a lesson about lying.

"I said try again!" The calm tone was gone, erased

by rage. She could feel the man's hot breath against the side of her head, the skin of her arm breaking under the pressure of his fingernails.

The sound of a dog barking penetrated the room, and the man abruptly loosened his grip and shoved her back down into the chair. As he crossed to the other side of the room, Katherine glanced around her, looking frantically for something familiar. The room was actually a screened-in porch, she determined, connected to what looked like an old cabin. It was dark outside, and there were no streetlights. Her chest ached, and she realized she'd been holding her breath. Dear God, even if she managed to get away from him, where was she?

"Damned, good-for-nothing mangy mutts," he muttered as he crossed back to her.

Katherine recalled the sound of a barking dog the night she and Aaron had first kissed. A sick feeling crept over her as she remembered the shadowy figure she'd seen dart behind the shrubs that same night. Johnny Jacobs. The man's name came to her with such clarity that she jumped.

A surreal calmness washed over her. Aaron. His presence warmed her as if he'd entered the room, and she willed her thoughts to stay with him. Block the fear—that's what she would do. Block the fear with thoughts of Aaron.

"Now where were we?" Jacobs squatted down in front of her. "I believe you were about to tell me how you knew Owen Blake." He slowly traced the barrel of the gun against her upper thighs.

Say you're Internal Affairs.

Aaron's voice filled the room—or was it just in her head? She glanced wildly around her, then back at the unfazed expression on Jacobs's face.

Say you're Internal Affairs. A decoy.

A sob broke from her throat. Aaron was there. She was certain of it. "I hear you," she said loudly, forcing her gaze to remain on Jacobs.

"Good," Jacobs responded. "I'm all ears."

"I'm Internal Affairs." She spoke the words with a new confidence, and watched the expression on his face melt into disbelief, then fury. "A decoy."

"You're lying."

"Am I?"

"Bitch!" he screamed. He leaped up and began pacing in front of her. Finally he stopped and pointed the gun directly at her face. "So now what am I going to do with you, huh?"

Say you're wearing a wire. Aaron's voice was steady and clear in her head. She wanted to stop and question what was happening, but didn't. In her heart she knew she didn't have to.

"You won't do anything with me. I'm wearing a wire."

Jacobs laughed, throwing back his head to reveal a row of perfect white teeth. He looked like anything but a killer. Small-framed and short, he had thinning light brown hair and ordinary eyes. The kind of face you easily forgot, Katherine realized. The kind of face you looked right over when suspicions ran high.

His laughter ended abruptly, and he leveled a stare at her that made her blood run cold. "You're lying. Blake didn't have time to make good on his threats."

He smiled. "I told him blackmail was a good way to get killed, and I was so right. In fact, I was so right that I decided to prove it to him." He winked. "I'm always right."

Katherine responded with only a smile.

Jacobs cocked his head and looked at her intently. "No, you might be IA, but there's no wire."

Get ready. Aaron's voice was low.

Katherine crossed her legs and smiled. "Okay."

Jacobs's composure broke, as she'd known it would, and he sprang toward her like a rabid dog. "Stand up," he snarled as he hauled her to her feet. "Let's have a little look."

As she watched Jacobs reholster his gun, she understood. She scrambled back a step just as Aaron came crashing through the screen door.

"Drop it!" Aaron commanded as Jacobs reached for his gun.

The shot rang out in the split second that followed, and Jacobs fell to the floor. His body twisted uncontrollably, his left hand clutching his wounded right arm.

"Katherine—"

She watched as if in a dream, her gaze fixed on the pool of crimson that soaked the old wooden floor beneath Johnny Jacobs. Aaron cautiously moved forward and retrieved Jacobs's gun.

"Katherine?" She felt Aaron's warm hand slide into hers as he untied them. "Are you okay?"

"Yes," she whispered.

"Thank God." He kept his gaze and his gun on

Jacobs as he pulled her against his side and placed a gentle kiss on her temple.

"H-how did you—how did we—?"

A small laugh escaped him. "That I don't know." He pulled her tighter against him. "My God, I thought I'd lost you."

"Never." She buried her face against his chest. "I don't understand, Aaron. Why—why did he do this?"

"Do you want to answer the lady, Jacobs?" Aaron's voice was venomous, and Katherine felt his muscles tighten against her.

"Go to hell!" Jacobs spat the words.

Aaron took a steadying breath and tightened his grip on her. "Let's just say we've had a departmental leak." He nodded at Jacobs. "But I think we found it."

"How did you know what had happened?"

"You're at a lake cabin just outside of town. Owen Blake's cabin." Aaron didn't try to disguise the anger in his voice as he uttered the dead man's name.

Understanding surged through her. Johnny Jacobs had said he'd killed Owen Blake, had admitted that the other man had tried to blackmail him. But it hadn't dawned on her until now that the two had been partners. One outside the law, and one inside the police force.

There had been only one problem with the partnership: One of them had ended up dead. And there had been only one problem with the murder: She had known more than she was supposed to.

Katherine started to tremble as the realization of what had just happened sank in. She clung to Aaron, never wanting to let go. "How did you know he'd brought me here?"

He paused, and she felt him take a deep breath before answering. "I just knew," he said softly.

She felt her body awaken to the husky tone of his voice, but now was the time to prove her love with words instead of actions. She felt tears slide down her cheeks. "I love you, Aaron Stone," she whispered.

"I know."

When she looked up, Aaron was grinning down at her. "What, I can't know things too?"

Aaron replaced the phone in its cradle and turned to face her. "They've found it."

Katherine reached for his hand. Now they had the final proof. Finding Jacqueline's husband's car was the last hurdle, the last sad reminder of darker days. Those days were behind them now.

Aaron pulled her into an embrace, warming her body, her soul, with his touch. Though they sat on the same worn sofa she'd used every day for years, in the familiar surroundings of her apartment, Katherine felt a tremor of excitement, a sense of newness, run through her. Their whole lives stretched before them.

"I'm forever indebted to you," he whispered before leaning back to meet her eyes. "You've given me the truth." His eyes glistened as he stroked her cheek. "Hell, you've given me my life back."

She circled his wrist with her hand and lifted his palm to her lips for a kiss. "And you taught me how to look beyond the road beneath my feet."

Aaron pulled her to him for a kiss. "What's behind us will always be there. But we still have everything in front of us."

She smiled as a million sweet possibilities flashed before her. "Yes, we do."

"Katherine!" Grams's voice preceded a heavy pounding on the interior door that joined her apartment to Grams and Walt's downstairs.

Aaron and Katherine jumped apart like two guilty teenagers. She paused to wipe a smudge of lipstick from his mouth before answering. "Come on in."

"I declare, child." Grams shrieked as she barreled through the door and into the living room. "We leave you for a week and look what happens. If not for Cheryl, we wouldn't even have known what happened—"

"I'm sorry, Grams. I asked Cheryl to get in touch with you. I didn't want you to see it on the news."

Grams pulled up short, glancing from Katherine to Aaron, then back again, completely ignoring Katherine's apology. "You must be him."

Aaron threw back his head and laughed. "God, I hope so!"

Walt joined them, and Katherine thought she saw Aaron's eyebrows quirk slightly. She'd spent so much time around Walt that his clothes no longer startled her. Today, though, his choice was jolting by anyone's standards. He wore a violet-and-yellow-plaid shirt, paired with kelly-green golf shorts.

Katherine leaned toward Aaron and whispered, "He refuses to believe that he's color-blind."

Aaron smiled, then stood and extended his hand

toward Grams. "I'm Aaron Stone." Katherine watched Grams return Aaron's handshake with her usual steely grip.

Walt shook Aaron's hand as well before scooping her up in a hug. "Hey, Gypsy," he said loudly. "What's all this I've been hearing?"

Tears sprang to her eyes as she returned Walt's hug. "It's been some vacation."

Walt had always been there when it mattered, calling her his beautiful Gypsy princess, bandaging skinned knees, and scraping together money for whatever she needed. And, she recalled, lending her a shoulder when some gangly teenage boy broke her heart.

"Cheryl tells me I get to say 'I told you so.'" Grams crossed her arms across her ample chest when Katherine didn't answer. "I'm talking about your gift, your abilities."

Katherine glanced at Aaron. Even after all they'd been through it was difficult to admit to anyone else. And even more difficult to say out loud.

Finally she nodded. "I guess I've just been afraid to look too closely at what was happening, at why I knew the things I knew." She closed her eyes and took a deep breath, then opened them to meet Grams's perplexed stare. "The truth is, I was afraid of ending up unstable like my mother."

"Unstable?"

She nodded. "Mental illness stole my mother from me. I've been afraid all my life of ending up that way."

Grams literally gasped. "Whatever gave you that idea, child?"

"What do you mean?"

Grams squared her shoulders and stared straight at Katherine. "I mean your mother wasn't mentally ill. That's what I mean."

Katherine looked from Walt to Grams. "But I remember the visions. She used to see things—things and people that weren't there."

Grams only shook her head. "What you remember, love, is that your mother was sick." She reached out to draw Katherine nearer to her. "Don't you see? She wanted to spend every moment she had with you, refused to go to the hospital and be separated from you."

"But I remember—"

Grams pulled her into a fierce hug, stroking the back of Katherine's neck as if she were a child again. "You remember the effects of the medicine, not mental illness. I'm so sorry." She rocked them back and forth as she spoke. "How could they—how could we—have not explained it to you?"

"Don't you dare apologize." Katherine pulled back to meet the older woman's gaze. "You and Walt gave me everything. Do you hear me? Everything I needed."

Walt stepped forward, a serious expression on his face. Katherine felt a stab of fear. She had never seen her foster father look so nervous—so grim. He reached into his pocket, retrieved his wallet, and fished out a scrap of yellowed paper. "I have something for you. It's long overdue, but I think you're finally ready."

Katherine felt Aaron's arm wrap around her shoulders as she reached for the paper. Written in a strangely familiar handwriting was her father's name, along with a telephone number.

Walt cleared his throat. "I can't say I've ever forgiven him, honey. He left you behind, and that's something I can't even imagine." He nodded toward the scrap of paper. "I don't think he knew any other way, with his work taking him on the road and all. He sent that to me when you first came to be with us, asked me to give it to you if I ever thought you were ready." He glanced at Aaron, then back at Katherine. "I think you're ready."

Katherine felt an undeniable calmness, a strange peace. She stared at the phone number for a moment, then looked at the circle of people who stood before her. She felt the strength of Aaron's fingers against her shoulder, the warmth of his body next to hers. The strange connection that had brought them together had transformed, grown into an undeniable bond of love. One that would tie them together forever.

She smiled and closed her eyes as she spoke out loud. "I remember my mother—her soft hands, the way she smelled of soap and lotion as she tucked me in at night. And I remember my father. He used to bring me Moon Pies and little packs of peanuts when he came home from the road."

Finally, she realized, after all these years, the memories didn't cause her pain.

When she opened her eyes again she focused on the faces of her foster parents. She saw the love shining from Walt's eyes, and sensed Grams's unwavering strength radiating toward her.

"You know what we need?" Grams wiped away an uncharacteristic tear, then waved her hand with an air of authority. "A nice cup of chamomile tea, that's what."

Katherine glanced at Aaron. A mischievous smile played across his face as he leaned toward her. "I dare you," he whispered.

"Uh—Grams . . ." Katherine fought to contain the laughter that threatened to overtake her.

"What is it?" Grams narrowed her eyes and glanced from Aaron to Katherine. "You two look like the cat that ate the canary."

"Well . . ." Katherine conjured up her sweetest smile. "There is something I've been meaning to tell you. . . ."

EPILOGUE

Katherine slid the dresses into the clear plastic bag and secured the bag at the bottom with a knot. She accepted the check from the woman, then smiled at the teenage girl who stood next to her. "You take good care of those for me. They're originals."

The girl, who had worn a pained pout since arriving at the charity sale, looked suddenly interested. "You mean no one else has one like them?"

"Not a soul."

The older woman eyed her suspiciously, took a second look at the dresses, then bustled away as if Katherine might change her mind.

Cheryl plopped down in the chair next to her. "I see your customers are still leaving in a huff."

Katherine threw up her hands. "I didn't even do anything that time!"

Desiree arrived with a box bigger than she was.

"More donations," she announced as she set the box on the table.

A tremor of excitement ran through Katherine. She and Aaron had formed the plan to build a shelter for battered women and children, with nothing but desire and intuition to guide them. And now, a year and countless fund-raising efforts later, Safe Haven was a little closer to becoming a reality.

"Excuse me. Excuse me." Aaron's masculine voice parted the sea of female browsers. He came to a stop before her, panting as if he'd just run a marathon, her black velvet evening gown clutched in his hand. "I just bought this off a very disagreeable woman for a very disagreeable sum of money."

Katherine stared at the dress. "Why?"

"Why? What were you thinking, putting this dress in the sale?"

"I thought the dresses would be a good addition to the fund-raiser." Katherine placed her hand over her rounded abdomen and was rewarded with a serious kick. "And I was thinking that, between the baby and your cooking, the waistlines on my dresses deserve better."

"Don't tell me you put them all up for sale."

"I want a new beginning." She smiled and rolled her eyes. "Hey, I want closet space."

"Well this one's not for sale." Aaron dropped to his knees beside her and planted a kiss on her growing belly. "Besides, you'll want to show the dress to our daughter when she asks about the night her mommy and daddy first . . ."

Katherine raised her eyebrows.

Aaron actually blushed. "What *are* you going to tell her?"

Katherine smoothed a strand of hair from Aaron's forehead, then leaned down to whisper in his ear. "What else? I'll tell her that her daddy was a dream come true."

THE EDITORS' CORNER

It's hot in the city! And in the country. And in the North. And in the South. And in the mountains. And at the seashore. And . . . well, you get the picture. It's just plain hot! Don't worry though, Loveswept's September loot of books will match the sultry weather out there. Even the air conditioner won't stop these characters from sizzling right off the pages and into your homes!

Devlin Sinclair and Gabrielle Rousseau are walking **ON THIN ICE,** LOVESWEPT #850, Eve Gaddy's novel about two attorneys bent on taking on the world and each other. Thrown together through no wish of their own, Devlin and Gabrielle must defend a reputed crime boss—a case that could ultimately make their careers, involving a man who could ultimately ruin Gabrielle's life. Devlin knew there was more to his sinfully gorgeous partner, especially since he accidentally bumped into her in the Midnight and Lace Lingerie shop! Annoyed that Devlin looked as if he'd guessed her wildest secrets, Gabrielle had to struggle not to melt when the charming rogue called her beautiful. But sometimes, in the heat of denial, one can discover heat of another kind. Eve Gaddy's romantic adventure pairs a fallen angel with a man who's her match in all things sensual and judicial!

In **AFTERGLOW,** LOVESWEPT #851 by Loveswept favorite Faye Hughes, professional treasure hunter Sean Kilpatrick is about to meet her match when she joins forces with Dalton Gregory in the search for a legendary cache of gold, silver, and priceless jewels buried somewhere on Gregory land. When Dalton comes to town to oust Sean, who he's sure is just a slick huckster on the make, he finds a copper-haired beauty whose enthusiasm for the project quickly becomes infectious. Sean is stunned by her intense attraction to this gorgeous, yet conservative history professor, but when he agrees to help chase a fortune, close quarters may not be all that they share. Spending more time together only accentuates the slow burn that is raging into a steady afterglow. Faye Hughes tempts readers with the ultimate treasure hunt in a tantalizingly steamy romantic romp!

Cheryln Biggs tells a deliciously unpredictable tale about the **GUNSLINGER'S LADY,** LOVESWEPT #852. There's a new girl in town in Tombstone, Arizona, and Jack Ringo aims to find out just what she's doing sprawled in his cactus patch dressed up in petticoats—especially since the Old West Festival doesn't start until tomorrow! Kate Holliday can't understand why Johnny Ringo is dressed up in strange clothes and without his guns, but the man was definitely as dangerously handsome as ever! Jack is quickly bewitched by Kate's mystery, frustrated at her existence, and inflamed by the heated passion of a woman who may disappear with the dawn. Adrift in a world she'd never imagined, uncertain of all but one man's need, can a sassy adventuress find her future in the arms of a man who couldn't guarantee the coming of tomorrow? Cheryln Biggs delivers a timeless love story that dabbles in destiny and breaks all the rules!

Loveswept newcomer Pat Van Wie adds to our lineup of delectable September romances **RUNNING FOR COVER,** LOVESWEPT #853. When Deputy Marshal Kyle Munroe shows up at Jennifer Brooks's classroom door complete with an entourage, Jenny knows that her time of peace and security is long gone. Jenny is reluctant to trust the man who had once shunned all she had to offer, but deep down she knows that Kyle may very well be the only one she can truly count on. Threats against her father's life also put hers in danger and the reluctant pair go into hiding . . . until betrayal catapults them into a desperate flight. And once again, Kyle and Jenny are faced with the same decisions, whether to find safety and love together, or shadows and sadness apart. Sizzling with sexual tension and the breathless thrill of love on the run, Pat Van Wie's first Loveswept explores the joy and heartache of a desire too strong to subdue.

Happy reading!

With warmest regards,

Shauna Summers Joy Abella

Shauna Summers	Joy Abella
Editor	Administrative Editor

P.S. Look for these Bantam women's fiction titles coming in August. *New York Times* bestseller Tami Hoag's breathtakingly sensual novel, **DARK PARADISE,** is filled with heart-stopping suspense and shocking passion. Marilee Jennings is drawn to a man as hard and untamable as the land he loves, and to a town steeped in secrets—where a killer lurks. Another *New York Times* bestselling author, Betina Krahn, is back with **THE MERMAID,** a tale of a woman ahead of her time and an academic who must decide if he will risk everything he holds dear to side with the Lady Mermaid. Dubbed the queen of romantic adventure by *Affaire de Coeur*, Katherine O'Neal returns with **BRIDE OF DANGER,** her most spellbinding—and irresistible—novel yet! Night after night, Mylene charmed the secrets out of men's souls, and not one suspected that she was a spy devoted to the cause of freedom. Until the evening she came face-to-face with the mysterious Lord Whitney, a man who will ask her to betray everything she's ever believed in. And immediately following this page, preview the Bantam women's fiction titles on sale in July.

The newest novel in the enthralling, passionate Charm Bracelet Trilogy . . .

"Jane Feather is an accomplished storyteller . . . rare and wonderful."
—*Daily News of Los Angeles*

THE SILVER ROSE

by Jane Feather

author of *The Diamond Slipper*

Like the rose in the haunting tale of "Beauty and the Beast," a silver rose on a charm bracelet brings together a young woman and a battle-scarred lord . . . Ariel Ravenspeare has been taught to loathe the earl of Hawkesmoor and everything he represents. Their two families have been sworn enemies for generations. But it's one thing to hate him, and another to play the part her vicious brothers have written for her—trapping Hawkesmoor into a marriage that will destroy him, using herself as bait. Forced into the marriage, Ariel will find her new husband unexpectedly difficult to manipulate, as well as surprisingly—and powerfully—attractive. But beneath the passion lurks the strand of a long-hidden secret . . . a secret embodied in a sparkling silver rose.

Ranulf stood at the door to the Great Hall. He stared out over the thronged courtyard, and when he saw Ariel appear from the direction of the stables, he descended the steps and moved purposefully toward her. She was weaving her way through the crowd, the dogs at her heels, a preoccupied frown on her face.

"Just where the hell have you been?" Ranulf demanded in a low voice, grabbing her arm above the elbow. The dogs growled but for once he ignored them. "How dare you vanish without a word to anyone! Where have you been? Answer me!" He shook her arm. The dogs growled again, a deep-throated warning. Ranulf turned on them with a foul oath, but he released his hold.

"Why should it matter where I've been?" Ariel answered. "I'm back now."

"Dressed like some homespun peasant's wife," her brother gritted through compressed lips. "Look at you. You had money to clothe yourself properly for your bridal celebrations, and you go around in an old riding habit that looks as if it's been dragged through a haystack. And your boots are worn through."

Ariel glanced down at her broadcloth skirts. Straw and mud clung to them, and her boots, while not exactly worn through, were certainly shabby and unpolished. She had been so uncomfortable dressing under the amused eye of her bridegroom that morning that she had grabbed what came to hand and given no thought to the occasion.

"I trust you have passed a pleasant morning, my wife." Simon's easy tones broke into Ranulf's renewed diatribe. The earl of Hawkesmoor had approached through the crowd so quietly that neither Ranulf nor his sister had noticed him. Ariel looked up with a flashing smile that betrayed her relief at his interruption.

"I went for a drive in the gig. Forgive me for

staying out overlong, but I drove farther than I'd thought to without noticing the time."

"Aye, it's a fine way to do honor to your husband," Ranulf snapped. "To appear clad like a serving wench who's been rolling in the hay. I'll not have it said that the earl of Ravenspeare's sister goes about like a tavern doxy—"

"Oh, come now, Ravenspeare!" Simon again interrupted Ranulf's rising tirade. "You do even less honor to your name by reviling your sister so publicly." Ariel flushed to the roots of her hair, more embarrassed by her husband's defense than by her brother's castigation.

"Your wife's appearance does not reflect upon the Hawkesmoor name, then?" Ranulf's tone was full of sardonic mockery. "But perhaps Hawkesmoors are less nice in their standards."

"From what I've seen of your hospitality so far, Ravenspeare, I take leave to doubt that," Simon responded smoothly, not a flicker of emotion in his eyes. He turned to Ariel, who was still standing beside him, wrestling with anger and chagrin. "However, I take your point, Ravenspeare. It is for a husband to correct his wife, not her brother.

"You are perhaps a little untidy, my dear. Maybe you should settle this matter by changing into a habit that will reflect well upon both our houses. I am certain the shooting party can wait a few minutes."

Ariel turned and left without a word. She kept her head lowered, her hood drawn up to hide her scarlet cheeks. It was one of her most tormenting weaknesses. Her skin was so fair and all her life she had blushed at the slightest provocation, sometimes even without good reason. She was always mortified at her obvious embarrassment, and the situation would be impossibly magnified.

Why had Simon interfered? Ranulf's insulting rebukes ran off her like water on oiled leather. By seeming to take her part, the Hawkesmoor had made a mountain out of a molehill. But then, he hadn't really taken her part. He had sent her away to change as if she were a grubby child appearing unwashed at the dinner table.

However, when she took a look at herself in the glass in her chamber, she was forced to admit that both men had had a point. Her hair was a wind-whipped tangle, her face was smudged with dust from her drive through the Fen blow, and her old broadcloth riding habit was thick with dust, the skirts caked with mud. But she'd had more important matters to attend to than her appearance, she muttered crossly, tugging at buttons and hooks.

Clad in just her shift, she washed her face and sponged her arms and neck, before letting down her hair. Throwing it forward over her face, she bent her head low and began to brush out the tangles. She was still muttering to herself behind the honeyed curtain when her husband spoke from the door.

"Your brothers' guests grow restless. I don't have much skill as a ladies' maid but perhaps I can help you."

Ariel raised her head abruptly, tossing back the glowing mane of hair. Her cheeks were pink with her efforts with the hairbrush and a renewed surge of annoyance.

The hounds greeted the new arrival with thumping tails. Their mistress, however, regarded the earl with a fulminating glare. "I have no need of assistance, my lord. And it's very discourteous to barge into my chamber without so much as a knock."

"Forgive me, but the door was ajar." His tone carelessly dismissed her objection. He closed the door on his words and surveyed her with his crooked little smile. "Besides, a wife's bedchamber is usually not barred to her husband."

"So you've already made clear, my lord," Ariel said tightly. "And I suppose it follows that a wife has no rights to privacy."

"Not necessarily." He limped forward and took the brush from her hand. "Sit." A hand on her shoulder pushed her down to the dresser stool. He began to draw the brush through the thick springy locks with strong, rhythmic strokes. "I've longed to do this since I saw you yesterday, waiting for me in the courtyard, with your hat under your arm. The sun was catching these light gold streaks in your hair. They're quite delightful." He lifted a strand that stood out much paler against the rich dark honey.

Ariel glanced at his face in the mirror. He was smiling to himself, his eyes filled with a sensual pleasure, his face, riven by the jagged scar, somehow softened as if this hair brushing were the act of a lover. She noticed how his hands, large and callused though they were, had an elegance, almost a delicacy to them. She had the urge to reach for those hands, to lay her cheek against them. A shiver ran through her.

"You're cold," he said immediately, laying down the brush. "The fire is dying." He turned to the hearth and with deft efficiency poked it back to blazing life, throwing on fresh logs. "Come now, you must make haste with your dressing before you catch cold." He limped to the armoire. "Will you wear the habit you wore yesterday? The crimson velvet suited you well." He drew out the garment as he spoke, and looked over at the sparse contents of the armoire. "You appear to have a very limited wardrobe, Ariel."

"I have little need of finery in the Fens," she stated, almost snatching the habit from him. "The life I lead doesn't lend itself to silks and velvets."

"The life you've led until now," he corrected thoughtfully, leaning against the bedpost, arms folded, as he watched her dress. "As the countess of Hawkesmoor, you will take your place at court, and in county society, I trust. The Hawkesmoors have always been active in our community of the Fens."

Unlike the lords of Ravenspeare. The local community was more inclined to hide from them than seek their aid. But neither of them spoke this shared thought.

Ariel fumbled with the tiny pearl buttons of her shirt. Her fingers were suddenly all thumbs. He sounded so assured, but she knew that she would never take her place at court or anywhere else as the wife of this man, whatever happened.

"Your hands must be freezing." He moved her fumbling fingers aside and began to slip the tiny buttons into the braided loops that fastened them. His hands brushed her breasts and her breath caught. His fingers stopped their work and she felt her nipples harden against the fine linen of her shift as goose bumps lifted on her skin. Then abruptly his hands dropped from her and he stepped back, his face suddenly closed.

She turned aside to pick up her skirt, stepping into it, fastening the hooks at her waist, trying to hide the trembling of her fingers, keeping her head lowered and averted until the hot flush died down on her creamy cheeks.

If only he would go away now. But he remained leaning against the bedpost.

She felt his eyes on her, following her every move, and that lingering sensuality in his gaze made her blood race. Even the simple act of pulling on her boots was invested with a curious voluptuousness under the intentness of his sea blue eyes. The man was ugly as sin, and yet she had never felt more powerfully attracted to anyone.

A new novel from one of the most appealing voices in Southern fiction . . .

"A uniquely significant voice in contemporary women's fiction."
—*Romantic Times*

A PLACE TO CALL HOME

by Deborah Smith

author of *Silk and Stone*

Deborah Smith offers an irresistible Southern saga that celebrates a sprawling, sometimes eccentric Georgia family and the daughter at the center of their hearts. Twenty years ago, Claire Maloney was the willful, pampered child of the town's most respected family, but that didn't stop her from befriending Roan Sullivan, a fierce, motherless boy who lived in a rusted-out trailer amid junked cars. No one in Dunderry—least of all Claire's family—could understand the attraction. But Roan and Claire belonged together . . . until the dark afternoon when violence and terror overtook them and Roan disappeared from Claire's life. Now, two decades later, Claire is adrift and the Maloneys are still hoping the past can be buried under the rich Southern soil . . .

I planned to be the kind of old Southern lady who talks to her tomato plants and buys sweaters for her cats. I'd just turned thirty, but I was already sizing up where I'd been and where I was headed. So I knew that when I was old I'd be deliberately *peculiar*. I'd wear bright red lipstick and tell embarrassing true stories about my family, and people would say, "I heard she was always a little funny, if you know what I mean."

They wouldn't understand why, and I didn't intend to tell them. I thought I'd sit in a rocking chair on the porch of some fake-antebellum nursing home for decrepit journalists, get drunk on bourbon and Coca-Cola, and cry over Roan Sullivan. I was only ten the last time I saw him, and he was fifteen, and twenty years had passed since then, but I'd never forgotten him and knew I never would.

"I'd like to believe life turned out well for Roanie," Mama said periodically, and Daddy nodded without meeting her eyes, and they dropped the subject. They felt guilty about the part they'd played in driving Roan away, and they knew I couldn't forgive them for it. He was one of the disappointments between them and me, which was saying a lot, since I'd felt like such a helpless failure when they brought me home from the hospital last spring.

My two oldest brothers, Josh and Brady, didn't speak about Roan at all. They were away at college during most of the Roan Sullivan era in our family. But my two other brothers remembered him each time they came back from a hunting trip with a prize buck. "It can't hold a candle to the one Roan Sullivan shot when we were kids," Evan always said to Hop. "Nope," Hop agreed with a mournful sigh. "That buck was a king." Evan and Hop measured regret in terms of antlers.

As for the rest of the family—Daddy's side, Mama's side, merged halves of a family tree so large and complex and deeply rooted it looked like an overgrown oak to strangers—Roan Sullivan was only a fading reflection in the mirror of their biases and regrets and sympathies. How they remembered him depended on how they saw themselves and our world back then, and most of them had turned that painful memory to the wall.

But he and I were a permanent fixture in local history, as vivid and tragic as anything could be in a small Georgia community isolated in the lap of the mountains, where people hoard sad stories as carefully as their great-grandmothers' china. My great-grandmother's glassware and china service, by the way, were packed in a crate in Mama and Daddy's attic. Mama had this wistful little hope that I'd use it someday, that her only girl among five children would magically and belatedly blossom into the kind of woman who set a table with china instead of plastic.

There was hope for that. But what happened to Roan Sullivan and me changed my life and changed my family. Because of him we saw ourselves as we were, made of the kindness and cruelty that bond people together by blood, marriage, and time. I tried to save him and he ended up saving me. He might have been dead for twenty years—I didn't know then—but I knew I'd come full circle because of him: I would always wait for him to come back, too.

The hardest memories are the pieces of what might have been.

On sale in August:

DARK PARADISE
by Tami Hoag

THE MERMAID
by Betina Krahn

BRIDE OF DANGER
by Katherine O'Neal